A BEAST WITHOUT A NAME

A BEAST WITHOUT A NAME

*Crime Fiction Inspired
by the Music of Steely Dan*

EDITED BY BRIAN THORNTON

Down & Out Books
3959 Van Dyke Road, Suite 265
Lutz, FL 33558
DownAndOutBooks.com

The characters and events in this book are fictitious. Any similarity to real persons, living or dead, is coincidental and not intended by the author.

Cover design by Damonza

ISBN: 1-64396-043-1
ISBN-13: 978-1-64396-043-2

CONTENTS

FOREWORD
Bill Fitzhugh

By the age of ten I was a devotee of Top 40 AM radio and was collecting records—45s by The Box Tops, The Temptations, Tommy James and the Shondells. It was the best of Top 40 AM radio because that's all there was. But soon the FCC forced license holders of AM/FM stations to broadcast original programming on the FM band.

Owners didn't know what to do, so they let some enterprising hippies into the studio to play all that crazy new music they were listening to along with blues and Elvis and somebody else's favorite song.

Thus was born FM rock radio. No static at all.

Only one problem: cars didn't have FM receivers at the time. So we bought FM converters or 8-track players that picked up the signal. (Can you say Blaupunkt?) And we put speakers in the back. We never knew music could sound so good as we tooled around our little hometowns.

The timing was cosmic. Millions of music-loving kids coming of age, graduating from bubble-gum stuff squawking from a paper-thin speaker in the dashboard to the new FM stations playing everything from Jimi Hendrix to The Allman Brothers to Kraftwerk, in glorious stereo no less.

It was a planetary alignment leading to Steely Dan. Sure

they had a couple of Top 10 hits on AM radio, but for the most part their songs were too sophisticated (and too long) with obtuse lyrics and jazz influences. They wouldn't play "Do It Again" on AM until they cut two minutes out of the thing. I was fifteen when *Can't Buy a Thrill* was released. I had it on 8-track and wore it out. By the time I was a senior in high school I had a decent album collection and I was working the 10 p.m.-to-2 a.m. slot on WZZQ-FM, a 100,000-watt FM rock station in my hometown. I worked in radio off and on for the next fifteen years and I kept collecting albums, including everything by Steely Dan.

Flash forward to the late 1980s and I'd been out of radio for ten years and had turned to the writing dodge. Moved to Hollywood to do sitcoms. That didn't work. Tried screenplays. Couldn't sell one. Decided to write a novel. While casting about for the name of the protagonist for that first book (*Pest Control*), I settled on the name "Bob" and kept writing. Eventually I needed a last name and I went with "Dillon."

Bob Dillon.

Hilarity ensued. Or at least some harmless fun. I sprinkled the story with little bits of lyrics, song titles, and trivia from that other Bob. They had nothing to do with the story or plot or character; they were just gags. "Easter eggs," my editor called them.

This device was well-enough received that I did it again when writing my second book (*The Organ Grinders*), featuring protagonist Paul Symon and antagonist Jerry Landis. You either get that or you don't, and it's fine either way. You can always look it up.

For my third book (*Cross Dressing*), I named my protagonist Dan Steele, as in Steely Dan. I lifted names from the Dan's catalog for the characters in the story: a nun named Sister Peg, and a hooker named Josie. A couple of gang members called Razor Boy and Charlie Freak. And somewhere in there, a character could be found contemplating that ditch out in the

2

Valley they were digging just for him. Little Steely Easter eggs hidden throughout the text.

The idea of a collection of crime stories inspired by the songs of Steely Dan seems natural, almost obvious, and definitely overdue. What is Steely Dan if they're not jazz-rock noir? The songs are populated by characters with shady pasts, dubious presents, and doomed futures. Sometimes they tell stories, other times just sort of suggest a dark tale, the details left to the listener's imagination.

Over the course of thirty years, Walter Becker and Donald Fagan created their own universe, chock full of gamblers, junkies, and the occasional pedophile. What might happen if you co-mingle the occupants of this world? Do the Whiz Kids know the Show Biz Kids? Are you disturbed by Cousin Dupree's skeevy look or the dreary architecture of his soul? Perhaps one of the writers in this collection will get him together with Mr. LaPage and an 8-millimeter camera. You say Katy lied? Then what happened? Did it involve the Third World Man? The possibilities are endless, as evidenced by the collection you have in your hands.

You can't buy a thrill? I beg to differ.

INTRODUCTION
Brian Thornton

An anthology is, by definition, a group effort. *A Beast Without A Name* is no exception. I have many hands to shake, many high-fives to award, and much thanks to give.

First of all, to our contributors: aces, every one of them. So nice to have twelve talented people send you their absolute best. So daunting to try to do that superb work justice during the editing process.

Next to Eric Campbell, Lance Wright, and the rest of the fun, friendly folks at Down & Out Books. "Supportive" doesn't even begin to describe it.

And of course, to David B. Schlosser, Stacy Robinson, and Jim Thomsen. Your assistance with the edits was invaluable from start to finish. *A Beast Without A Name* is so much the better for all of your input.

And lastly, to my wife, Robyn, and our son, James. Your patience, good humor, insights, and support while I worked on this project have meant the world to me.

Thank you all!

PIXIE DARE RETURNS
Peter Spiegelman

"You know your problem?" he'd asked Jane, but he didn't want her answer. He had one of his own, and was proud of it—eager to show it off. Like a puppy with a stick, she thought. An old, jowly puppy—doughy, with a shaggy moustache, wooly eyebrows, and salt-and-pepper hair too long on the sides, and gone up top. He wore tweed and a stained necktie. "Your problem is the male gaze," he said, smiling, waiting for something—a laugh maybe, or applause. She saw nicotine stains in his moustache.

"No shit?" Jane had said. "And all this time I was sure it was the male dick." She smiled back and brushed the auburn bangs from her green eyes.

She could tell right away that she'd missed something— that he'd been hoping for a different response, something more specific and appreciative—but she knew he was tickled just the same. His raspy laugh was real, and he leaned across the library table and put out a hand.

"I'm Armie," he said.

It was like a supermarket chicken—pale, soft, cool and damp, the flesh thin over the bone. She saw him glance at her ragged nails, the grit around them, the burns and cuts on her knuckles, and she fought the urge to hide her hands up her coat sleeves.

"Jane," she said. His eyes were brown and warm—puppy eyes—but also bloodshot and clouded. Hungover puppy? Sad puppy.

She'd seen him before in the reading room, not every day, but most days since she'd walked out of Port Authority and taken refuge there. He was always at the same table, and always had a stack of books in front of him—massive slabs, ancient, with pages like cobwebs. Maybe he was trying to conjure something.

Jane had seen him watching her sometimes, though not only her. He'd watched lots of people—was curious about them. A snoop. *A real yenta*, Mrs. Fischel would've called him. Mrs. Fischel was herself a real yenta, and an endless bitch besides. A million years ago, she was a neighbor lady down in Tampa, in the trailer across the way from Jane, her mom and her latest fake step-dad. A million years? It'd only seemed that long. Jane had been in NYC barely three weeks that day.

Armie didn't always watch her, but he'd been watching just then, when that bearded dude hit on her. *You a student, baby? Where you at school? NYU? Whatcha studyin'? You study hard?* The guys were different and so were the lyrics, but the tune never changed. The boredom and exhaustion of listening to it was the unstated price of admission to the library. Still, it was better than the street, Jane knew. Warmer. Drier. Fewer guns. There was comfort in the quiet and the musty smell. And that mile-high ceiling—like some crazy dream. You could wander off into those clouds.

Armie had watched her with beardy-dude, as he'd watched her with other guys before. Watched the way she could slide and pivot from their attentions, smile, glide, play them for a coffee, or ice them from the jump. Beardy-dude was frozen before he'd said word one.

Armie squeezed her hand, leaned closer and smiled wider. "You need lunch, Janie?" he asked. "A sandwich, maybe?" She caught a whiff of coffee breath, and cigarettes.

* * *

Jane's head jerked, and bumped the glass. The warmth of sunlight on the window bench, and the smell of coffee, wafting from her mug, had set her drifting. The metallic squeal of the UPS truck, pulling up in front of the brownstone, had brought her back.

The driver climbed from the truck, legs winter white in his uniform shorts. He tucked the box under his arm and took the stairs two at a time. His round, acne-scarred face was eager. It was Paul.

Jane sighed and worked up a smile. She opened the front door before he rang, leaned a hip against the doorframe, swung her blond ponytail back, crossed her arms, pushed her breasts up against the fabric of her black tee, and gave him a grin. Paul smiled, tried not to stare, tried to focus instead on his package scanner, but it was an uphill fight.

"Hey, Gretchen."

"Hey yourself, Paulie. Nice wheels, you're sportin'. But you seriously think spring is here? In March?"

A blush rose up Paul's neck. "Take it from me, it's time to stow that puffy coat."

Jane shook her head. "I love your optimism, babe."

"I save it for you."

Paul was toast even without the breasts, Jane knew. She'd been working him since October, when she'd moved in with Donald—had joked and fist-bumped all through the dark winter, with Paulie, Steve, Rasheed and a platoon of nameless holiday temps. Even when Donald took the deliveries, or Cleo, his ill-tempered Dominican maid did, Jane had been at the door, smiling, saying hi, stroking her ponytail. By February, Cleo was seeking new opportunities, and Donald wasn't taking packages. But as long as Jane smiled and fist-bumped, nobody asked questions about signing, or why so-and-so hadn't been around, or about anything at all. The breasts were just extra dazzle—some after-burn on the retinas, like when a flash goes off, to make sure there wasn't too much blood going to Paulie's brain. Jane waved as he drove off, then carried the box to the second floor parlor that she'd turned into shipping and receiving.

She'd drawn the drapes across the windows, dragged the Barcelona chairs and coffee tables to the walls, and rolled up the rugs. In the center of the parquet floor was her inventory. Handbags, wallets, belts, shoes, scarves, outerwear, and more shoes—Italian, English, French, some American brands, even a few Japanese and Swedish names—all designer, all authentic, and nothing under four figures, full retail.

She pulled a butterfly knife from the pocket of her cargo pants, spun it, and slit the box. It was the Prada bag, in candy-red calf leather, with chrome hardware and studs. $2,200, plus tax. She placed the Prada in a row with the other handbags, and tossed the box in a corner with the empties.

Jane closed the knife and scanned her stock, recalculating its value. A cost base of $78,500, with a liquidation value of approximately $54,300. On the one hand, a 31% loss didn't make for a great business model; but on the other, none of the seventy-eight-five was hers, and all of the fifty-four-three would be. So there was that.

Jane sat in one of the Barcelona chairs and yawned—money stuff always made her tired. She'd learned a lot from Armie, but not about finances, so she was making it up as she went: asset liquidation, maxing out credit lines, moving money, laundering it. She somehow made it work, even if she still left lots on the table. And with each go 'round she improved—digging deeper into deep pockets, hauling up more every time.

With the guys Jane had gone for early on, money mechanics hadn't been an issue—there was always lots of cash around. But there was a downside to drug traffickers, she'd learned: they tended to raise a ruckus. She ran a finger over a scar down her right forearm, and thought of Georg. Tall, dark, pretty enough, in a pouty, Eurotrashy way—though not enough to make up for the meanness, or the fact that, beneath his heavy cologne, he always smelled like unwiped ass. She'd since refined her type. Now she went for older guys, successful but past their primes—past the first mid-life crisis, but poised for the next. Guys who would be flattered and grateful; guys in search of an audience, a student, a muse.

Armie would've been tickled, she thought, that she was managing the financials—tickled and surprised—and Jane would've liked to see that. It usually went the other way with him: Armie was the one full of surprises.

Starting with lunch, that first day. Jane had been halfway certain that *lunch* meant a hotel room, and *sandwich* meant blowjob, but she'd been wrong. Armie took her to a deli on Seventh Avenue, and after she'd demolished her pastrami on rye, and half of his, he asked where she was from. She'd owned up to Tampa, but the rest of her story was bullshit, and she was pretty sure Armie knew it. On their way out of the deli, he bought her a roast beef on a hard roll, and a cream soda.

"Can't live on pastrami alone, Janie," he said, as they walked back to the library. "Gotta broaden your horizons."

The next day, he had a reading list for her, and a stack of books in the spot opposite his at the big table. Laura Mulvey, Wendy Arons, bell hooks, John Berger, Sherrie Innes, Angela Carter, Judith Mayne. Film theory, feminist theory, lit crit, popular culture, economics, politics, history. Jane felt vaguely nauseated, but along with the books, Armie had a proposition.

"You read, and I buy lunch. Breakfast and dinner too, if you want. But you gotta read."

Jane smiled. "How're you gonna know I'm reading, and not just drooling? That's how I spent most of school."

Armie smiled back. "Because we're going to talk, over

lunch or breakfast or whatever, and you're going to tell me what you make of it all."

"Like a book report? I don't do homework."

"Not homework. More like conversation."

Jane shook her head slowly, but she'd picked a book from the stack, and sat.

The doorbell rang and Jane shook her head, and struggled to remember who she was supposed to be. She went to the front windows and peeked down at the stoop.

"Fucking Melanie," she whispered.

Melanie Metz lived in a building that backed onto Donald's garden. She'd had a petition on clipboard when Jane first met her—something about a condo blocking sunlight—and she wanted Donald's signature. Jane was pretty sure that she also wanted Donald. But though Melanie was attractive—with gray-blond curls, a wide mouth, and a tight yoga bod—Jane never worried. Melanie was maybe fifty—about Donald's age—and so was twenty-five years too old for him.

Jane read the jealousy and suspicion in Melanie when they first met, and made adjustments—dialing down the sexy, dialing up the awkward and artless. A little sister who needed a big sister's help to make sense of the charming pirate. Gretchen's dewy-eyed naïveté had eroded some of Melanie's hostility, but a residue remained, and Melanie continued to circle and yip, like an annoying Pekingese.

"What now?" Jane muttered, and headed downstairs. Along the way, she mussed her hair, stretched her T-shirt into a baggy tent, and donned a round-shouldered slouch.

"What's up, Mel?" Jane said, smiling.

"Hello, Gretchen," Melanie said, coolly. "Is Don back yet? I wasn't sure from Facebook when he might be around, and I wanted to talk about this housing fundraiser I'm doing. People on my committee would love to get Susan Sarandon for the dinner, and Don said he knew a guy." Melanie craned her neck as she spoke, and tried to look over Jane, into the hallway and beyond.

"I'll ask, but he barely answers my texts. One time in five maybe."

Melanie nodded, peering into the house. "He's still in Argentina?"

"Uruguay, I think."

"'Til when?"

Jane shrugged. "'Til he's done researching his script. *Research*—I think he's just eating steak and drinking wine."

Melanie scowled. "Meat—ugh. He must be shopping too. I see UPS and FedEx and DHL here *all* the time."

Jane slowed her breathing, relaxed the muscles in her face, and shrugged again. "I know, right—seems all I do is answer the bell."

Melanie nodded. "You here by yourself?"

"Yup." Melanie was still trying to summon her X-ray vision when Jane closed the door.

"*Shit*," Jane whispered. Fucking social media—she'd forgotten to post. She should've figured Melanie would be following Donald. *Shit.* That's what happens when you stay too long—*yentas.*

Jane checked her watch. She'd post on Donald's Facebook after midnight—after the last FedEx pickup, and after she'd read up on tourist highlights of Uruguay. She'd name-check some of those, throw in some bullshit about cultural dislocation and jetlag, douse it in a quart of self-regard, and hopefully sound enough like Donald to allay Melanie's suspicions. It'd worked so far.

Upstairs, boxing four pairs of Jimmy Choos, Jane thought about Melanie's snooping, and flashed on Armie, in those first weeks of her studies. She remembered him gazing across the library table—all but walking around to read over her shoulder.

* * *

For the first couple of weeks, things had gone as advertised: with Jane reading, and Armie feeding—two, sometimes three meals a day. But besides watching as Jane studied, Armie didn't try to discuss anything. He'd waited until week four for conversation.

As promised, it was nothing like school. There was nothing for Jane to parrot, no *compare and contrast*. What Armie wanted to discuss was what Jane thought of living in a world that was organized by straight white men, for the benefit of straight white men—a world in which a woman's value was determined by her labors for these men—how thoroughly she slaked their appetites, how subtle the balm and bolster she provided to their bottomless vanity. Armie had actually said it that way—*balm and bolster*—and it was a good thing they were eating lunch in Bryant Park when he did, as Jane had spit cream soda across the bench.

"Congratulations on your discovery that water's wet!" she said, laughing. "You're a genius." Armie was crestfallen, but Jane went on. "Really—you think this is news to anyone?" Armie's puppy eyes drooped, and Jane tried to swallow her chuckles. "Okay, okay—I see you're serious. You really want to know what it's like—I'll try to explain. I think it's kinda like...dog shit on the sidewalk. If you see it coming, you step around; if you don't, then you scrape your shoe. Either way, you move on."

Armie thought about that as he ate his chicken salad. "You make it sound like an *annoyance*—an irritation, but ultimately a minor one."

"Major or minor depends on how good you are at spotting those turds, no? Otherwise, it's a lot of shoes."

"Wouldn't it be better to live in a world without dog shit?"

Jane sighed. "How're we gonna manage that—by killing dogs? People wouldn't approve."

Armie drank soda and thought for a while. "Some women don't have a problem with the whole situation. They embrace it, and exploit it."

"You mean they've *internalized* it? Become *complicit*? Maybe you tell someone dog shit is ice cream for long enough, she might start to buy in. Enough time, you might get her to say *yummy*, and ask for an extra helping. Also, try not to look shocked when I use words like *internalize* and *complicit*—it's kind of insulting. I may not have read this crap before, but I know *how* to read."

It was Jane's turn as the puppy with the stick then, and Armie's turn to laugh appreciatively. Proudly even.

Jane skinned tape across three of the boxes. She was about to seal the fourth when she froze, dropped the tape gun, and moved to the windows that overlooked Donald's garden. She drew aside the drapes.

There were shadows on the brick paths, and on the shrubs along the brick walls. A wind passed through the branches of the Japanese maple, and made it fidget like a nervous suitor. What had she heard? A cat? A garbage can? Nothing? Just her own nerves. Which is another thing that happens when you stay too long.

"Fuck it," Jane whispered. She'd ship these packages tonight. By tomorrow morning she should have four more sales easy, and by tomorrow night she'd draw the line. Whatever she had then is what she'd have, and she'd pack up regardless. She'd hop a subway to Rego Park, and hoof to her storage locker. She'd take care of her hair, her clothes, her phones there, and that would be adios, Gretchen. She took another look at the garden, then closed the drapes.

Patsy was driving for FedEx that night, and her vast apathy was a relief. There could've been body parts in those boxes, for all Patsy cared, and Jane could've sprouted another head.

The only words they exchanged were *hey* and *later*, and Jane was deeply grateful. She had just locked the front door when her phone chimed a reminder. Jane checked the screen and saw a single word: *Pixie*.

Shit! She'd nearly forgotten: there were three episodes tonight, on TBS—a three-hour block of *Codename: Pixie Dare*. They started in ten minutes, which was barely time enough.

Jane sprinted to the kitchen, tossed a bag of popcorn into the microwave, and grabbed a couple of bottles of orange soda from Donald's fridge. Then she took the stairs two at a time to the third-floor master, and Donald's king bed and sixty-five-inch television. She kicked off her boots, nestled the popcorn bowl in her lap, hit the remote, and let the music send her.

How had she lived so long without having heard of Pixie? Armie sometimes joked it was because all of Florida was benighted, and Tampa especially. Mostly, though, he attributed it to Pixie's nearly two-decade absence from the public's view— fallout of the long legal wrangle over the show's syndication. *Another way Noah Corso found to fuck me*, Armie would invariably add. Which didn't explain how Jane had missed the meticulous online episode guides, the kinky fan fiction, the obsessive 'shippers who droned on endlessly about every conceivable romantic permutation of *Pixie* characters. As it happened, when Jane finally found Pixie Dare, it wasn't Armie who made the intro, even though it was from his head that Pixie—Venus in body armor—had sprung.

Jane was four months into the list when it happened, and she and Armie had found a comfortable rhythm of reading, eating, and arguing about whatever came to mind—the role of particular film editing techniques in establishing the primacy of the male perspective maybe, or gender differences in spectatorial pleasure, or—a favorite subject of Jane's—the tortured style of some academic writing, and the tendency of certain authors to disappear entirely up their own asses. And then she reached the final volume in the stack—a collection of essays on feminist models in late-twentieth century popular culture—and an article entitled *Buffy and Pixie: Third Wave Feminists or Just More T&A?*

"What the *fuck*, Armie?" she whispered, tapping the page with an index finger. "This is *you* they're writing about."

He looked up from his own book and smiled blandly.

"Who the hell is Pixie Dare?" Jane said.

Armie rose, picked up his coat, and headed toward the exit. Midway, he looked back and crooked a finger.

Aside from that first lunch, their relationship had, until then, existed only within the bounds of the main branch of the New York Public Library, on the paths and benches of Bryant Park, and on the landscape of their conversations. All else was *terra incognita*, and *don't ask, don't tell.* So Jane had no idea of where or how Armie lived, or what he did for money, and was never asked those questions herself. Still, it didn't occur to her not to follow. They did not return to the library.

Not that they went far—only by subway to Clark Street, in Brooklyn Heights, and then to a townhouse near the corner of Willow and Pineapple that Armie had bought with part of the pile *Pixie* had made for him in its seven years on primetime. The house was blue clapboard, sagging and peeling, and inside it smelled like Armie—of coffee, cigarettes, booze, and age.

He took her through the dim front hall, past a parlor full of lumpy furniture, and up a narrow staircase. His office was on the second floor. There was a Mac on the oak desk, and Armie switched it on and clicked the Netflix icon.

"All seven seasons are there," he said. Then he trudged down the stairs. Jane looked around for a moment, took her backpack off, sat at the edge of a swivel chair, and clicked on *season 1; episode 1*, the eighty-six-minute pilot.

That was the first time she heard the music—the jazzy, smoky, brushed snare and hi-hat heavy theme that Jane eventually learned was called *Pixie's Run*, but that right then and there burrowed deep into her breath and blood. And then the titles—in dark blues, greens and purples, on an ink-black background—an animated silhouette, stylized, angular, but unmistakably female, leaping, twisting, cartwheeling across a nighttime cityscape, and in acid yellow letters, across the top of the screen—*Codename: Pixie Dare*. Executive producer Armand Del Vecchio. Created by Armand Del Vecchio. Written and directed by Armand Del Vecchio.

The pilot laid it out. Pamela "Pixie" Deering, top high-school athlete, scholar, and wholesome-but-sexy girl next door, becomes a teen superspy when her father and mother, physicist Simon and engineer Nina, perish in an apparent sailing accident, and Pamela is recruited by the same secret intelligence agency that employed them. The Defense Authority Directorate is headed by Pam's Uncle Rupert, known as U, who oversees her training—a punishing six-minute montage of Pam running, jumping, fighting, shooting, driving, skydiving, safecracking, and donning disguises. After which she's issued her mother's arsenal of miniaturized weaponry, her father's tricked out Shelby Cobra, and the codename Pixie Dare.

All the members of Team Pixie—her steadfast ground crew and surrogate family—were introduced in the pilot too. Besides imposing U, there was maternal Jessica Roth, the directorate's operations chief, gruff Commander Gomez, head of the tactical division, brilliant-but-eccentric Dr. Witz, the technology guru, and her teenage son, Randall, an awkward computer prodigy, hopelessly smitten by Pixie.

Jane barely moved through season one—once to take off her coat, and once to pee—and she moved not at all through seasons two and three. Armie brought her a turkey sandwich and a soda at the start of season 4, by which time she was crushing harder than Randall.

Pixie—the name still made Jane sigh. Was there anything she couldn't do? Certainly the spy stuff was no sweat. Pixie kicked ass barehanded, and with anything at hand—a stapler, yogurt, whatever. The same with disguises: Pixie went from slinky to sporty to geek to goth in a blink. The driving, diving, swooping were similarly a breeze—slo-mo daydreams, with that blond ponytail streaming like a pennant, and Pixie smiling like a pageant queen. Even the tribulations of her student cover life didn't trouble Pixie. The mean girls, nosy guidance counselors, and disastrous dates were played for laughs, and Pixie brushed them off like lint. All of that made Pixie watchable fun, but it was her focus that made Pixie special.

Whether executing U's assignment of the week, or untangling the conspiracy behind her parents' deaths—a six-season-long arc—Pixie was a laser beam, a diamond drill, a bullet hole: never distracted or deterred. And when things went south, as they often did, Pixie would improvise—boldly, recklessly, but always locked on the goal. From abandonment and loss came cold resolve; from grief, purpose—it was heady stuff, and it turned Jane's crush into something else.

Casting helped there. Blond, blue-eyed, pro-surfer Sara Muir brought intelligence and humor to Pixie's teenage snark, and unexpected pathos to her cool competence. But it was Sara's physicality that made Jane's heart race. She was tall, narrow-hipped, and broad-shouldered—a boyish, athletic frame, like Jane's own. When she moved, it was with a dancer's speed and fluency. When she struck, she was a hammer. And those freckles...

The theme music faded on the TV, and commercials played, and Jane ate popcorn and drank soda. When the episode resumed she groaned. It was late *Pixie*—episode nine from season seven— the season after the season where Pixie discovered the secret of her parents' deaths; the shark-jumping season with the musical episode and the Christmas special; the season where Pixie and Randall finally, implausibly, get together—implausibly because it was clear after season four that Pixie was gay, and yearning for Magda Singh, Commander Gomez's taciturn lieutenant. Season seven: the one-too-many season; the one where former story editor Noah Corso became the showrunner, and wrote and directed most of the episodes; the one where Sara Muir—barely nineteen when the pilot filmed—began to show her age and her boredom; the first season after Armand Del Vecchio's departure. The last season. The bad one.

Of course, even bad Pixie was Pixie, and so Jane watched—a mindless tale about industrial espionage at a toy company, with a B-story about too many prom dates—and ate popcorn, and thought about Brooklyn.

It was good for her there. Better than the library, because she didn't have to hide in an A/C duct at closing, or bathe in a bathroom sink. In Brooklyn, at Armie's place, she had her own room, with a bathroom and nice morning light. Plus Armie gave her cash for whatever, and asked no questions. He gave her more books to read, too, and a list of movies and shows to stream, and the file boxes with all his *Pixie* scripts, and chuckled at her fan-girl enthusiasm. But when Jane dyed her hair, and started dressing like Pixie, in camo cargo pants, black tees, and Doc Martens, Armie didn't laugh or say a word, but just smiled blandly.

That was a good time for him, too. He cleaned the house, cleaned himself up, cut back on the booze, and went for walks with Jane along the Promenade. And he would talk to her—endlessly—about her reading, her viewing, and of course about Pixie. Jane wanted to know everything, and Armie obliged. From story ideas to casting decisions to fight scenes and special effects, he opened every kimono. Or, almost every one.

Try as she might, Jane couldn't pry loose the story of Armie's departure from *Codename: Pixie Dare*. Nor could she get him to explain what the fuck happened in season seven, how the show plummeted into farce from the stunning season six finale, in which Pixie learns that her Uncle—the inscrutable, infallible U—was in fact the man behind her parents' death, that he'd been manipulating her since day one at the directorate, that her career there was mostly a lie, that Rupert was evil in ways she never imagined, and in which Pixie exacts a righteous, purifying revenge. Jane cajoled, whined, badgered, but Armie turned sad puppy, and kept mum.

But Jane, like Pixie, was focused. And if Armie was silent, the internet wasn't. It took some digging, through stories about creative differences and contract disputes, and too-plausible rumors about Armie's drug and alcohol problems, but finally Jane hit pay-dirt: some early-90s' photos of Armie at the Emmys, the People's Choice Awards, a Bill Clinton fundraiser. He was cute, with dark, curly hair, a bushy porn 'stache, no belly, and a vibe of rumpled cool. And on his arm—hell, all *over* him—was tanned, leggy, freckly Sara Muir.

More digging revealed that they'd been a couple, from the end of season one until sometime in season six. After which Armie basically vanished, while Sara went bigger and better: the female lead in three faux-*Die Hard*s, the female lead in three sort-of-*Runaway Bride*s, two seasons as the headliner on a CBS sitcom, and four in a police procedural on USA. By which time the internet was a thing, and social media too, and Sara—a mother of two by then—deftly reinvented herself as the face of a mommy lifestyle brand, with a blog, a YouTube channel, massive Facebook and Insta footprints, and a line of yoga clothes. Jane confronted Armie with her research.

"She goes by Sara Muir *Corso* now, Armie. As in Mrs. Noah Corso."

Armie looked up from his laptop with the same bland smile she'd seen in the library. His voice was soft. "They've been happily married for twenty years, or so says her Facebook page."

"Is that what happened? You two were a thing, then you

split, then she took up with Corso and you quit the show?"

He shrugged. "Sort of."

"*Sort of?* What the fuck does that mean?"

Jane bit on an unpopped kernel and winced. Episode nine from season seven was over, and episode ten began—an even stupider story about a runaway kid who stumbles on the directorate's underground headquarters. Jane spit the kernel across the room, and it bounced against the screen, and then her eyes flicked to the rear windows. What had she heard? Something outside? She rolled off the bed and went into the bathroom. She shut the door, left the lights off, and went to the window. It was black now, and it took her eyes a moment to adjust. She stood motionless in the dark, looking into the garden. The shadows were deeper, moving with the wind. But one patch did not. Jane stared at it.

That was almost their first fight—Jane demanding an explanation; Armie digging in. Finally he relented—beaten puppy. His voice was low and tired.

"We were together for four years. *Engaged*, for chrissakes."

"So what happened?"

"I fucked it up. But I had help."

Jane squinted at him.

"I had help from booze and blow and a barely legal PA."

"So, you cheated on your fiancée, and she dumped your ass. Sounds like you deserved it."

Beaten puppy vanished for an instant, replaced by a beast Jane hadn't seen before—angry puppy. "You don't know shit about people. You don't know what it's like—"

"You're saying it *wasn't* your fault?"

"It wasn't *only* my fault. Noah knew about my problems, and the pressure I was under—I wrote every *fucking* episode!

And he knew about the morals clause in my contract. He *put* me in the way of that fucking PA, who I know he hired for exactly that purpose: to be in *that* booth, in *that* dress, at *that* hour, with two shots of tequila, two grams of Peruvian flake, and some bullshit about her mean boyfriend. Fucking Chateau Marmont—the money I dropped at that place over the years..."

Jane shook her head. "Boo-hoo. You're saying the bar was out to get you too?"

"It's a hotel—and screw you. Somebody arranged for a photographer to be there, and somebody let him in, and I'm pretty sure of who did what. And I *know* who sent Sara those pictures the next morning." Armie made a snuffling sound, and tears rolled into his quivering moustache. The sight of it made Jane's mouth tremble.

"Corso did all that?" Jane said after a while. "He set you up that way, like a target?"

Armie sniffed and nodded. "He set me up, but Sara was the real target. He wanted her—he always had. When she got those photos, he was there with a shoulder. And a couple of weeks later, he was there with a whole package of deals— taking the show in a different direction, films for her, that he'd produce, a network deal...He'd been working on that stuff for a year before, I found out. It wasn't a month before they moved in together."

"Jesus. You tell her what was going on?"

"There was video, too, from that night. Sara didn't want to hear my voice after that."

"And the final season, the show turning to shit?"

"Noah's brilliant vision."

"What a fucking *prick*," Jane said softly.

Armie laughed. "Worse still, it was my idea." Jane squinted again. "You remember season three, episode seven?" Armie asked.

"The honey trap!" Jane said. "Fuck, yes—what Corso did was *just* like that."

He nodded, and smiled blandly.

Armie turned sullen in the days after his confession, and Jane thought he was angry with her. "What the hell's your problem?" she said, standing over him. "You pissed 'cause you told me that stuff?"

Armie shook his head. "I'm mad because I can't have peace, even in my own town." He was at his dining room table, staring into his laptop, and he turned it so Jane could see.

It was the New York Comic Con website, and a schedule of panel sessions and speakers. Armie pointed at a Saturday morning entry: *Girl Power 2.0—Female Superheroes in the Post-#MeToo World*, and atop the list of panelists: *Noah Corso—producer, director, writer; creator and executive producer of* Domino Danger.

Armie's voice was tight with anger. "I always go to Comic Con," he said. "Now that that bastard is there, I can't go near the place." He pushed his chair back, went to the kitchen, and came out with a bottle.

"What's *Domino Danger?*" Jane asked.

"A series he's doing for CW," Armie said, "a shameless rip-off of *Pixie.*" Then he poured a tumbler-full of bourbon.

Jane breathed slowly in the darkness, lowering her heart rate, waiting. When a figure moved from the Japanese maple toward the house, Jane moved too.

There were four days until the Comic Con panel, which was plenty of time for Jane to blow up Noah Corso's shit: to find his hotel—a place downtown; to get friendly with a waitress in the lounge there, learn that he was staying alone, and learn his tastes in single malts, amongst other things; to observe him at a midtown screening of the *Domino Danger* pilot, at the Q&A afterward, and at a Tribeca bar later, where he pawed a twenty-something publicist until she ran, pale and weeping, into the rain.

Corso was thick, and twice Jane's size, with eyes like pea gravel, skin like a worn basketball, a graying two day scruff, and a brush cut too young for him by thirty years, despite his dye job. He looked like a poorly barbered bear, Jane thought, with anything endearing hacked off, and only the surly, hungry, hunting parts left.

He looked worse naked, as Jane learned the next night, when he brought her—dragged her really—to his hotel suite. Getting there was ridiculously easy: Jane went full Pixie cosplay, which was basically her daily garb, sat in his sightline in the hotel lounge, and ordered a Macallan. Corso was on his third one of those, and Jane barely had to speak beyond *hi*.

Setting up the camera was easy too—Corso was too busy donning his bathrobe to notice. But the grappling was deeply nauseating. Corso smelled old and sour, his hands were like asphalt, and, Jane quickly realized, her resistance—each *no* and *stop* and *I don't want this*—only stoked his thrill and violence. It didn't go on long, though. In mere minutes, Jane's shirt was torn, and Corso was clutching her throat, grunting—*bitch, cunt, whore*—as he rubbed a vacillating erection on the thigh of her cargo pants. When she'd captured enough of this sweet talk, she spun open the butterfly knife she'd bought for the occasion, and pressed its needle point into his scrotum. Corso froze and held his breath, and his semi-boner became a garden slug.

"No means no, asshole," Jane whispered.

She was in the crowd at the Javitz Center the next day, and uploaded her video as the panel began. It rippled through the audience not ten minutes later, just as Corso was babbling about *Domino Danger* being his love letter to the amazing women who'd made him a better man. By the end of the day, the CW had pulled the show from its lineup, and ended its relationship with him. The following day, Sara Muir announced that she would file for divorce.

* * *

Jane was quiet down the stairs, to the garden level of Donald's house. She made the trip in darkness and stood on the bottom step and watched a flashlight beam cross the barred windows.

At first, Armie had had the dazed look of a lottery winner, desperate to believe the ticket in his hand, but not daring to. He watched and re-watched Jane's video on-line, and devoured the reactions, especially clips of the audience at Comic Con— an ululating chorus of catcalls and derisive laughter. When a reporter rang him for comments, Armie was measured and considered in his censure, never actually mentioning Corso's name. But Jane, watching him on the phone, saw him beam. He looked at her and mouthed *thank you.*

After that, Armie was transformed: he grinned, glowed, sang in the shower, and danced down the stairs. Suddenly he wanted to write again, to paint, to sail. But something about the butterfly troubled Jane. He smiled at her more, stared longer, stood closer. He wanted to take her to dinner, to hear music, off on a trip. Jane demurred. Instead, she returned to her reading, to some of the works Armie had first recommended, to the essay she hadn't gotten around to finishing: *Buffy and Pixie: Third Wave Feminists or Just More T&A?* She bought her own copy at The Strand.

After she'd read it, she walked on the Promenade and thought—about meeting Armie, the sad puppy, the angry puppy, that bland smile he wore sometimes, the essay...Then she went back to the house.

Armie was in the parlor, at his easel, and Jane threw the book at him. "Let's have a conversation," she said.

Armie ducked the book. "*Jesus*—what's wrong with you?"

"*An agent without agency,* the author calls her," Jane said. "*A burlesque of empowered femininity, scripted by a man, and performed by his puppet. A minstrel show."*

Armie picked up the book and scoffed. "Academics—heads firmly up asses. You said it yourself."

"Now I'm not so sure. Tell me, why did you talk to me that day in the library?"

"What?"

"Why? Why then? Why me? Were there other girls? Was the library the only place you went looking?"

He shook his head. "I don't know what you're talking about. Looking for what?"

"A puppet. Someone whose strings you could pull. Someone to put in Corso's way."

"You're cra—"

"Don't bullshit me, Armie. I've had enough from you."

He sighed and dropped into a chair. He was sad puppy for an instant, until he smiled blandly. Jane stepped forward and slammed a boot into the side of his chair. It toppled, and so did Armie.

"What the fuck!" he yelped.

"Don't show me that smirk again, shithead. It's your fucking tell—you do it when you're getting away with something. Now answer my question."

He climbed to his feet and brushed off his pants. "Which question?"

"Were there other girls?"

He stared at her for a while, and then smiled—wide and bright. "None with your potential. None as smart, or talented, or motivated. No one who could connect the dots like you. No one like you, Janie." Hearing him say it was like a hand at her throat. Armie took her wrist. She snatched it away.

"Don't be mad, Janie. Look what we've accomplished in just a few months. And we've barely started." He reached for her again, and she stepped back.

"Started what? What do you think we're doing? What do you think I am?"

27

Armie put a hand to her cheek, and whispered. "I think you're *something*, Janie—really *something*. Before, you were raw—just an angry cipher—but you've come so far now. Now, you're *amazing*."

Jane took a deep breath, felt her throat loosen. She laughed. "You can't hear them, can you—the words you're saying? You can't tell when you're plagiarizing yourself." Armie squinted. "From the season six finale—what Rupert says to Pixie when she confronts him: *You were nothing when you came to me—just an angry cipher. Now you have purpose— mission. Now, you're magnificent.* He says that right before he grabs her, professes his love, and tries to put his tongue down her throat."

The sad puppy was back, and Armie looked at his thread-bare brown socks. His voice was soft. "Of course I love you, Janie, and you love me. Don't act surprised—just look at what you've done for me. I didn't have to ask, or say anything— you knew what I wanted, what I needed, and you just did it. If that's not love—"

"You're making it worse, for chrissakes! Don't you know how pathetic you sound? How deluded?"

Sad puppy was gone, and angry puppy returned, angrier, colder than Jane had seen. She took a step back, and came up against the wall. Armie stepped closer, took her face in his hands, squeezed. "You little fucking b—"

There was a sliding metal *snick* and then angry puppy was gone for good, replaced for an instant by a new creature, who quickly flickered out too.

Surprised puppy. They always were, Jane had learned, when push came to shove. She moved quietly to the garden door, and quietly unbolted it. She stepped into deep shadow, spun out her knife, and waited for Melanie. Sometimes with yentas, as with bad dogs, it was the only way.

MONKEY IN YOUR SOUL
Matthew Quinn Martin

"You sick?"

"I don't think so," I managed to say, right before sneezing.

Joey folded her arms across her black uniform shirt and offered a knowing head tilt. "You're sick."

I shrugged. Maybe I was. Or maybe just allergic to something here. Who could tell, with all the dust and glitter and cleaning chemicals and God knows what else I'd been inhaling since taking this job a month ago.

"This is a good place to get sick."

She was right. An endless stream of kids pouring in and out from the moment we opened the arcade doors at 10 a.m., right up until we locked them at midnight. Rubbing their germs over all the stuffed llamas, the rag dolls, the action men. Shoving their hands into the candy bins. Pawing the comic books. It turned the prize redemption zone into nothing but a petri dish with toys floating in it.

She took a bite of the cheese sandwich she'd brought from home in a wax paper bag. Her default lunch, I'd come to notice. "Can go home if you want. I'll cover for you," she offered.

"That's not fair. You opened, and I'm supposed to be closing."

"Fair is a four-letter word."

"That's good," I said. "You should write that down."

The arms crossed again. The head tilted in the other direction. Even at twenty, Joey fell naturally into the role of den mother to those of us working prize redemption. Even me, and I was easily twice as old as her or any of the others. Maybe she had younger siblings. Maybe she just had that instinct. She'd make a good mother someday, if that's what she wanted.

She'd been here the longest too. Over a year in a position whose door, I'd been told, revolved faster than the spin-to-win game. Six employees fired in as many months. All, allegedly, for pilfering items from the glassed-in, high-end case—pricey things like video game consoles, or robot vacuum cleaners. High-end, but none worth more than a couple of hundred bucks.

I sneezed again. "No point," I told Joey. "Just be sick at home. Might as well get paid for it."

Her head stayed tilted. "Money's not worth your health. 'Specially not what they pay us."

She was right again. A dollar over the state minimum wasn't worth much more than covering groceries, barely. *Prize redemption is where souls go to die*, was what one co-worker told me right before she snagged herself a cocktail server position, escaping this particular metaphorical Gehenna.

But I was here for a different type of remuneration. Sure, counting reams of game tickets, stocking endless boxes of candy, and dragging around a fourteen-foot ladder to hang giant plush tigers wasn't exactly what I'd imagined for myself at this, the hinge of my life—if I'm lucky enough to have as many years left as those I've spent that is. But there's something priceless about the little things here. Like tossing a toy football back and forth with a foster kid who seemed shocked that you even asked what her name was. Or watching the anticipation in a kid's eyes as you drag that fourteen-foot ladder out of the back and pull down that stuffed tiger. To feel the sheer joy radiating as you hand it to them and bathe in that light just for a moment.

"It's fine. I'll be fine," I said, and sneezed again.

"Fine is also a four-letter word."

"That one's not as good."

We shared a small smile. It didn't last.

A loud, annoyed, "Fuck!" came from behind us. It played counterpoint to the thump of cardboard skittering across tile.

We turned to see Nando, one of the front-of-the-house managers, phone in hand, glaring at the stock boxes we'd spend the past hour or so breaking down.

"The fuck are these doing here?"

Joey instinctively scanned the prize redemption area for any parents we'd end up apologizing to for Nando's language. Thankfully, it was dead empty.

"New merch shipment today," I told him. "Those're headed out back."

"What? Waiting for 'em to grow legs?" Nando said. "Get 'em out of here."

Joey took a step forward to comply. I gripped her elbow. "I got it. Could use the air." I clutched one flap and started pulling the box-filled box across the arcade midway, toward the kitchen, heading, eventually to the compactor that abutted the mall's employee parking lot.

Nando followed. "You like her," he pronounced more than asked as he stole a look back at Joey. "You like her, don't you?"

I did, but not in the way he meant it.

"You got kids?" he asked.

"No."

"Still. Careful. That girl's young enough to be your daughter."

Not exactly. Six—eight—years difference, perhaps. As time slipped on, it was getting harder and harder to remember the specifics. And with that thought, a wave of shame roiled up inside me. I halted right in the middle of the midway, fist pressed to my chest, my breath a sucking wheeze.

"You all right, Cochise?"

"Little sick is all."

"Yeah. You look it." Not a trace of empathy in those glassy doll eyes of his. "Just don't go giving whatever you got to me, okay?" He slapped a meaty mitt on the boxes and started dragging them away. "I got it from here."

As I watched him disappear through the stainless saloon doors, I wondered why he even made me come with him this far if he was just going to take them out himself. But I was learning quickly that might just be how Nando was built. While the other managers all embraced, to varying extents, a corporate version of *the golden rule*, he preferred to do things old school. Passive-aggressive kidding on the square. Sisyphistic busywork. Petty punch-downs and perpetual ass-covering.

I remember one of my first closing shifts, he told me to take the garbage to the compactor on my way to my car, *after* I had punched out for the night. I pointed out that this was working off the clock—something I'd just signed paperwork affirming that I would not do. To that, he'd said *So?* And I told him, *So, that means I'm working for free.*

Just for like five or ten minutes was his response.

Which, admittedly, wasn't much when you were making just above minimum wage—and, still, *was* a hell of a lot when you were trying to live on such a wage. I'd be okay, myself. But Joey? How many cheese sandwiches was she going to miss out on because of this...theft, I guess? There really wasn't any other word for it. Petty theft.

Nando must have caught something in the way I looked off into the distance as I fired up the compactor. Something that didn't sit well. *What? You mad that you aren't getting paid for this?* He'd grinned. *Just think about all those people who get paid for doing nothing. It's got to add up someplace. That's just math.*

Yes. It all adds up. Where it always must. At the bottom.

Thankfully, if he'd said anything else, it was lost in the compactor's clanging hydraulic grind.

I turned from the memory, and found myself face to face with Albert, the arcade's senior game technician, and one of the few hourly employees older than I was. "You busy?" he asked.

"Not anymore."

"Good. Need an extra set of hands on the claw machine."

I followed him across the sprawling arcade to the back wall where the machine was located. With his fire-engine red tech uniform shirt and chest-length white beard, he looked a bit like Santa Claus's surly younger brother. Given the amount of toys he was responsible for dispensing, and the gruff way he went about it, that wasn't that far off.

"That guy giving you a hard time?"

"Who? Nando?"

Albert grunted in the affirmative.

"Not that hard."

"Horse hockey. And don't let that guy get to you. Ever since he started here, we been losing redemption staff left, right and center. And it's not just the missing merch that's making that happen. Don't want to see you as the next bit of collateral damage is all."

"Thanks."

"No thanks needed. It's not for you. Not a pep talk. It's survival. We need people in there. Smart people. Good people. You're clearly smart—"

"I don't know what you mean."

"Don't play dumb," Albert added sharply. "Too many dumb people wanting to play *smart*. Don't go trying to flip the script."

I half nodded.

"And you're good with the kids. Good with the parents too. Not a lot of folks can pull that off. Not in in a place where—"

"Souls go to die," I finished for him, not sure if those were going to be his next words or not.

"Yeah, yeah. Ha, ha. You know they call it *redemption* for a reason." Behind his bifocals Albert's eyes glistered. "I don't know what crazy gale blew you into this place, pal." He cast a quick glance to Nando, just now strolling back onto the midway. "Just don't let that windbag blow you back out. Hear me?"

Again, I half nodded.

Malik, another tech, and a computer science major at the local university, was waiting with the tool cart at the claw machine. The card reader's bezel flashed red, supposedly letting people know the machine was out of order, and rarely doing so effectively.

"'Sup," Malik said as I got closer, and offered a dap.

"Hey," I said as I accepted it.

Albert went straight for the cart. "Just grip the front panel on both sides," he said as he fitted a socket bit into his cordless drill. "Grip it good. That thing's heavy and the last thing I want is to spend the rest of the day cleaning up broken plate glass...and all your blood."

He wasn't exaggerating about it being heavy. It was a chore even holding the ungainly thing up as Albert fiddled around by the prize chute.

"Just as I thought," Albert said, holding up a bent steel flap. "Keep telling them we've got to move this thing where we can keep a better eye on it."

"What happened?" Malik asked.

"What always happens. Some jackalope. Some *drunk* jackalope, like as not, got frustrated that he couldn't beat a child's game to get a child's toy, decided the rules don't apply to him and did what any grown up who is used to getting his way does, he cheats. Shoves his hand in through the out door and fouls up the mechanism along the way." Albert *pinged* the flap with a flick of his middle finger. "Just ruining the fun for everybody after."

"Try straightening that out when you get back to the tech

office," he said to Malik as he dropped the flap onto the cart. It landed with a ringing clang. "Otherwise we gotta order a replacement. Machine's out of commission for a while, either way," he added. "Let's get the face back on and hang a sign up."

We repeated the process, just in reverse. Albert had just finished fastening the last bolt when he said. "Least it was just the flap this time."

"This time?" I asked, knowing there was more to the story, and knowing that Albert was a born raconteur who lived for stories. "How so?"

"Few years ago, opening shift, we came in to find someone'd pulled the same stunt. Guy who worked here cleaning up after hours. Difference was…he'd got stuck."

"Stuck?" Malik said. "How long?"

"All night. We found him there in the morning. Woke him up, actually." Albert took off his glasses and rubbed them with the hem of his shirt. "Boy did we laugh, me and the other tech working that day. He's not here anymore, the other tech. We figured we could get him out before the managers noticed, but were going to have a bit of funning along the way. Kept joking about how we were *probably* going to have to cut his hand off. Probably. You know, *hardy har har,* talk."

"And…"

"And. We got him out all right. And we didn't have to cut his hand off." Albert paused. Then his voice went far away and quiet. "No…the doctors did that. At the hospital."

Malik's own hand went straight to his mouth. "You're playing."

"Wish I was. That's just the cold truth of it. Watch band got caught on the flap, they said." Albert pointed to the bent flap still sitting on the cart. "And it acted like a…a…noose, something like that."

"Tourniquet," I said softly.

"That's it. Cut off the blood flow. Killed the hand straight dead, like what happened to that rock climber in that movie a while back. And that was that, no saving it. Jeeze Louise, think about it. Guy tries to steal a stuffed toy from the claw machine, ends up with a claw of his own for the rest of his life to remind him of that one dumb move."

Malik shook his head. "Man, that is some Jordan Peele's *Twilight Zone* shit right there."

"Watch. The. Language."

Malik's eyes scraped the carpet. This was obviously a discussion the two had had a few times already. "But why, man? Why do it?"

"People do a lot of dumb things," Albert said.

"Maybe he had a kid," I said. "Maybe it was for them."

Albert turned. "Could be. Nobody got to ask him, seeing how they fired him and all."

"Reminded me of a story, is all," he continued. "You know how they catch monkeys in Africa?"

"What? Like for the zoo and sh—uhh—stuff?"

"For whatever. The bushmen, they cut a hole in a coconut and tie a rope to it. Then they stick a piece of fruit inside and wait for the monkey to come get it. The monkey reaches inside and grabs the fruit. But then he can't get his hand out. The fist is too big for the hole. The bushman yanks the rope and...boom, monkey meat."

"Right...right," Malik snapped his fingers. "I heard that. 'Cept it was a baboon instead of a monkey. And it was salt instead of some fruit. And they put the salt in a hole in the ground instead of—"

"Missing the point here." Albert shook his head. "Point is, all the monkey had to do was let go. Just let go, and he'd have been free. But no, he just had to hold on."

"He held on," I said. "Because it was all he had. That's what you do when you don't have anything else."

Albert shook his head again. "You're missing the point too. Point is: don't be a monkey."

"Monkey," I echoed, looking through the glass front of the

claw machine at the pile of lifeless stuffed animals heaped inside. Looking beyond it and into a life that hadn't been mine for a very long time. "That's what we used to call my daughter."

Albert cocked his head in my direction. "Thought you said you didn't have kids."

I felt a twinge in my chest. I didn't remember telling him that. He must have overheard me talking with Nando. Not that it mattered. I just turned to him and said, "I don't."

Then I went back to redemption, and back to work.

"When can I see her?" my wife, Claire, asked from the other side of the Formica table.

It was a mistake coming here. A mistake I made, and would likely continue to make, every single Saturday from two to four p.m., during visiting hours.

"When can I see Rachel?"

She looked comfortable. Her pajamas looked reasonably clean. I wondered how long before the nurse would roll past with her little paper cups, pharmacy keys dangling from her wrist coil. "Soon," I said. "You'll get to see her soon."

And it wasn't a lie, exactly. And I think Claire knew that. I could see it in her smile. The same smile that always broadcasted who was controlling the transmission. It was a sign off, that smile. It was static.

Claire would see Rachel soon—slippery as that word could be. They'd be in the same place, wherever that was, soon, after a fashion. My wife was certainly determined to get there. That was plain enough. It didn't take a diagnosis from any of the doctors milling about to make it real. They'd be together soon. And no amount of counseling sessions, prescription pills, IV drips, or forced feedings were ever going to stop what Claire had started all those years ago when she let go of the emergency brake. When she did what put her here. What put Rachel where she was.

She nodded to the manila envelope sitting on the table. It was off to the side, but still somewhat between us. "What's that?" she asked, like she did every visit, every time she saw it, and never remembering. Her memory had been selective even before the *accident*, as the courts finally ruled it. But four minutes belted into a minivan, with two lungs full of icy river water—four minutes of being legally dead—made it so it was impossible to tell what was selective, and what was simply gone.

"Just paperwork," I told her, pulling the envelope towards me and slipping it into my shoulder bag.

"For your job?"

I offered a slight smile, but didn't answer.

"When can I see Rachel?"

"Soon," I told her, then looked at the wall clock encased in its metal mesh cocoon, a barricade to any soul looking for release at the corner of broken glass and vein. One hour and twenty-seven minutes to go.

Back in the car, I dropped the envelope in the empty passenger bucket. As always, it remained unopened. The divorce papers inside, unread and unsigned.

It's a myth that most marriages don't survive the death of a child. I've read that the actual percentage hovers somewhere around fifteen percent, well below the national average of people splitting up for reasons like infidelity or boredom. But I wonder, of those marriages that do survive, how many are like ours. And who, exactly, would look at that and call it survival.

I made a quick circuit of the prize-redemption area, broom and dustpan in hand, sweeping up errant candy wrappers, packing peanuts, and other detritus. Joey stood behind the counter, showing the ropes to another new trainee, one who would last six weeks if we were lucky.

I looked out to one of the massive monitors hanging over the bar. On it, a music video played. Another post-teen, post-

Disney pop star dancing the same robotic moves to the same synthetic beat they all did. Not that I could hear much of it. The music on the midway is punishingly loud, but for some reason it's almost inaudible here.

Despite the fully open arch that demarcated redemption from the rest of the arcade, it just fades to acoustic mud the instant you step over the threshold. I wonder what architectural wizard was able to pull of that sonic sleight of hand. I'd thank him if I could. I used to love music, but now the songs I know are all weighed down with too much memory. And the new ones just make me wonder what Rachel would have thought of them in a future that never happened.

As I pause to tidy up a bin of plush sloths, a little girl sidles up to me. She fishes one out, holds it at her tiny arm's length a moment for inspection, then hugs it to her chest. Hugs it like it's alive. Like it could somehow hug her back. They all do this, the kids. They do it all day. All of them. Gender never matters. Only age matters. And although there's no set cut-off date, at some point that connection, that craving is going to cease.

Another switch goes off. Another light goes out.

I read about a psychological study when I was in college. Some sick bastard had separated some infant rhesus monkeys from their mothers. Then he gave them the choice of a wire-frame with a bottle in its chest and a nipple to drink from—or one covered with fur that had eyes and a face, and nothing else. Without fail they went for the latter. They'd rather starve than live without love, or, at the very least, a simulacrum of such.

Once, after closing up, when there were no eyes to see me, I tried hugging one of the stuffed animals myself. I felt nothing. Not even foolishness. I suppose it only works if you are a child or a monkey.

I was just about done sweeping when I noticed an unopened box of rainbow Slinkys sitting upended beside the card reader. I picked it up and set it back under the display box where it belonged.

Or, at least, I tried to. A woman grabbed it from me just as I was sliding it home. "That's my daughter's." Her voice was pinched and mean, her face the same.

"The whole box?" I asked. There were two dozen of them inside. Even discounted as they were it would mean a lot of tickets.

She looked at me dumbfounded.

"Well, she can't want all of them, right?"

"What?"

I realized then that her daughter must have seen the ticket "price" sticker stuck to the side of the box and taken to mean that it meant the lot and not each individual slinky. And this woman simply hadn't noticed. I explained the situation.

"No, I don't want the whole box," she said after the reality of it sunk in. Embarrassment marbled her tone, adding a swirl of shame. But not the kind that speaks, *I'm sorry*—the kind that snarls, *How dare you make me look like that.*

"Well, here then…" I started, pulling one from the box.

"I don't want that. I don't want the box and I don't want that either. I don't want any of this." She gripped her daughter by the hand and her son by his upper arm, both tight enough to make them wince. "Come on. We're going." The children went along with her, silently if not willingly.

I wondered about her words. *I don't want any of this.* Did she mean the Slinkys? The rest of the trinkets? All the happiness swirling around her? The joy that wasn't hers? I only hoped that whatever demon was haunting her would leave her children be. But from the leaden look in their eyes as she dragged them to the door, I knew that hope was gossamer-thin.

Back at the counter I proceeded to pull a half-full trash bag from the can stationed at the side. "Taking this out," I told Joey.

She looked at the translucent bag and its meagre payload. "You still sick?"

I nodded.

"The cold?"

I shook my head and said, "Yeah." Then added, "Could use the air."

"I'll come with," she said. "Heading on break anyway."

I was about to protest when she added, "Trainee needs to get thrown to the wolves sooner or later. Only way anybody learns anything."

The air was brisk outside and a cold mid-March sun hung high in the sky, offering much light but no heat. I tossed the bag into the dumpster and sat down on the remains of an old brick planter. Joey leaned against the giant cardboard compactor opposite me. I gazed past her at the metal doors, weeping rust, at the back of the mall. The arcade, like most locations of the nationwide chain, was housed in the remains of an old "anchor store." A Sears, or a G. Fox, or some other chain that had long since gone belly up, leaving a cinderblock carapace for us to inhabit, like a hermit crab.

My eyes landed on a jumble of boxes next to the compactor. "You know, when I was a kid, all I ever really wanted was a big cardboard box."

"A cardboard box?"

"Yeah," I admitted. "I think about that sometimes when we're stocking toys. I'd live for the day when someone in the neighborhood would get a new refrigerator or a washing machine and then leave the box by the curb."

"That's sad," Joey said.

"Sad? How?" I asked, the earnestness, the honesty in her tone knocking me on my heels. "You know, a cardboard box could be anything. You just draw what you want on the outside with markers. It could be a race car, or a rocket ship, or a submarine. Cut hatches and portholes with a Stanley knife. How could something pure like that ever be sad?"

She absentmindedly kicked at a chunk of stray asphalt. "Because it's empty."

I tried to think of something to say—some response—and came up just as empty. I turned to head back in.

"Wait," she called just as my hand hit the handle.

"What is it?"

"It's Nando," she said, eyes off in the distance.

"What about Nando?"

"I think he's the one who's been stealing," she said. "Stealing the high-end stuff, the video games and whatnot, and pinning it on other people."

People working in prize redemption, she meant.

Joey flicked a glance to the cardboard compactor. "That's how he does it," she said. "He puts whatever he wants at the bottom of the empty boxes and then makes us take them out here. Then he comes back for whatever it is later. Pins it on one of us. Probably sells the stuff on eBay or gives it away to friends."

"But why? He makes four times as much as any of us."

"It's not always about money...you know that."

I did. And what's more, I didn't just *know*, I understood.

"Have you told the GM?"

"Don't have any hard proof. I tried to get it, but I think he knows I know...so he has other people do it, and...well, I think he's going to pin it on you next."

"Me? Why me?"

"Because you are a little too good at your job. Because, sooner or later, you were going to figure it out, even if I didn't tell you. People like you here. He needs to get rid of you before you can put down any roots, while you're still disposable." She looked to the dumpster, just to make her point all the more solid. "I can cover for you, if you want."

"What?"

"I can take the fall. You can let him pin it on me."

"Joey—"

"What difference does it make? I'm out of here in a couple months."

I raised an eyebrow and whether she noticed it or not, she continued.

"Graduating at the end of May and I'm moving to the city with my boyfriend. What do I care about getting fired from here?"

This was the first time she'd mentioned having a boyfriend. It was the first time she'd offered up a single detail of her personal life, honestly.

"Not like anybody gets arrested. Not like it's going on my permanent record. And…"

I waited, letting that *and* hang there until it found its way home to roost.

"And…I see you in there, in redemption, and it's not just a job for you, is it? It's some kind of calling. This place needs you. And…and I think you need it." She let out a trailing exhale, pluming in the late winter air. "Sure do a hell of a lot more than me."

"How is that any kind of fair?"

"What did I tell you about fair?"

I half nodded. A four-letter word.

I let what she said settle on me like heavy snow. Cold, but comforting. "Fine," I said as I wheeled for the door, vowing from now on to watch my language.

"Can I have a word?" I asked, poking my head into Nando's office.

"If this is about that cold," he said, not looking up from his computer screen. "Already told you I can't give anybody any time off."

I shook my head. "It's Joey."

"Don't tell me *she's* sick."

I shook my head again. "I think she's the one who's been stealing from the high-end cabinet."

Nando let out a quick half-laugh, right before pulling it back it. "What are you—"

"She's the only one who's been here the whole time it's

been happening," I said, just like she'd suggested I do. That I frame her. That I let her take the fall. "Makes more sense than four different people just up and getting the same idea after a few weeks of work." The words coming from my mouth tasted like ash.

"That's a serious allegation," Nando offered in his best fake *Law & Order* voice, all the time biting his lower lip. "You got anything to back it up?"

"I spotted one of the Nintendo Switches at the bottom of the cardboard boxes we were breaking down. I was going to say something, but then it was gone, and she was gone. They both were. I think she hid it in the boxes and took it to the compactor to get later. It think that's how—"

He rose fast enough to send his office chair careening to the back wall. "I'll handle this," he spat. "You get back to work. You hear me? Back to redemption."

I nodded as he buzzed past me, zooming straight for the parking lot. But I didn't go back to work.

I couldn't.

I was off the clock.

Joey and I had switched shifts. For all anyone but Nando knew, I was home watching the game.

I don't think he saw me. I saw him, sure, crawling into the open compactor door. I saw him disappear into a heap of cardboard, frantically digging for a three-hundred-dollar game console and the proof that finally might put his shenanigans to an end.

I don't think he saw me, and I don't think he heard me either, as I quietly slid the compactor door shut and closed the latch. And if he had time to scream, I didn't hear it. I don't know if that was because the machine was so loud, or because I just wasn't listening. And I don't care. Not even a little.

And I'm not sure how long it's going to take before anybody finds what's left of him. If the dump truck drivers are going to pay close enough attention to notice blood and brains oozing from another baled bundle. Maybe they never will. Maybe there was enough cardboard there to insulate the evidence, isolate him on his way to oblivion. And he'll be nothing more than a swiftly fading "Remember that guy who used to work here? Whatever happened to him?"

And I don't really care.

Well...maybe a little.

Tomorrow I'll be back in redemption, waiting for prizes of my own to appear. Waiting on all those little lights. Basking in the glow of all those borrowed candles...before time comes to blow them out.

It's all I have. And, monkey be damned, I'm not letting go.

HERE AT THE WESTERN WORLD
Naomi Hirahara

I am five-ten and weigh one hundred ninety-five pounds, average for a white male in America of my generation. I don't have much chest hair, but I do have some, which makes it convenient for adding and subtracting. The guys with the hairy chests often have to be shaved or be plucked, which at times can hurt as hell.

Here at the Western World, it really doesn't matter if you age, as long as your body stays average. I mean, you can be any extreme size you want, but you just won't be getting enough work. And since I'm a full-time grief surrogate, I need to be a blank canvas for the greatest number of persons possible.

Today's client has reserved me for an hour, so it will be an introductory session, almost a try-out. I sit naked in the padded makeup chair, a thin, crinkly paper underneath my ass. A rough white towel is placed over my lap. It really doesn't make sense for me to wear my briefs because I'll have to change out of them, anyway.

Ms. Lillie walks in and I let out a sigh of relief. She's my favorite liaison because she keeps the small talk to a minimum. This is just a job; we don't need to be best friends. She hands me an accordion folder. "It's a woman," she says.

I open the folder and read the name. It's only one word.

Felicity. Our clients never use their real names. There's a photo of her, an awkward selfie. She's Asian with long black hair and lips that seem to naturally pucker into the shape of an "O." I read about her circumstance, which is described very briefly. Her husband, Jim, died in a car crash a month ago. He was dark-haired with a square jaw. I can certainly be him.

Ms. Lillie brings over the mask of the face of the man in the photo. After lathering my forehead and cheeks with makeup adhesive, she positions it over my face. The husband had a more prominent nose and bridge than I do. And I've always wanted a strong jaw.

Since this is our first meeting and may be our last, I don't get my hair dyed. Instead Ms. Lillie pulls my hair into a skull cap and outfits me in a wig. While she is trimming and styling, I put some ear buds from the folder in my ears. I hear Jim's voice. They are all voicemail messages. His voice is low and self-assured. I think that I hear a tinge of the Midwest in them and I go back to his bio. He was raised in Kansas City.

While I'm in Ms. Lillie's chair, I practice his voice. "Hello, it's Jim. Remember that we have that work dinner tonight. Wear that red dress I bought you in Vegas."

Ms. Lillie keeps trimming and styling the wig fastened to my head. She doesn't compliment me on my attempt to get the deceased's voice right. She has a job to do, and I have mine.

After she's finished with my hair, she hands me a clear plastic bag with a snap top. I see a blue button-down shirt, dark jeans, white T-shirt and plaid boxers. I get out of the chair and change. Ms. Lillie has seen me naked at least four hundred times, so I've lost all self-consciousness.

The jeans are a tiny bit loose but there's a belt. I feel like I'm cheating by tightening it to the next inside hole. But it's just a first meeting. Ms. Lillie hands me a pair of socks and black dress shoes. Those surprisingly fit well, but when I take a few steps in the shoes, it's a reminder that Jim's natural gait is completely different than mine.

Ms. Lillie positions me in the mirror and I stare into the face that she's pulled together. "You're ready," she says and then pulls off the paper from the chair.

After I leave the Transformation Room, I encounter Dan in the Waiting Room, naked except for a towel around his waist. He's in his forties, the next category up in our average white man division. Sometimes I get his customers and he, mine. They come to me to imagine their partners in younger, perhaps happier times.

He immediately knows it's me and greets me by my name. If you've been in this surrogate game for more than a year, you learn to see underneath the mask.

I nod.

"Who do you have?" Dan tries to sneak a peek at my file. He's a nosy one and somewhat competitive. We do have an employee-of-the-month contest and I've won perhaps two times more than him. He's not going to quit until I show him.

"Oh, an Asian girl. They are the best," he says, leafing through Felicity's accordion file. "Not so much tears and the sex is great."

I've had my share but I've found they are actually a mixed bag. I've had older ones who want to imagine their husbands or partners when they first met them. Sometimes they just want to cuddle and talk but other times they want the sex fast and furious, remembering how it used to be.

"Have to go. My appointment is at two," I pull the accordion file out of Dan's hands.

"Yes, you definitely don't want to be late for this one," he calls out. I leave the waiting room for the hallway leading to the reunion rooms.

I recheck my paperwork. Reunion Room Number Six. That's a good one. A corner one that even has some views of the city.

Like all the rooms, it's furnished with a Victorian-looking couch with red velvet padding. And then a table with two chairs facing each other. I place the file on the table and then gaze out of the window at the tops of buildings and the stop-and-go traffic below.

There's a knock at the door and I quickly turn, positioning my body straight towards the doorway.

"Fuck," Felicity says as soon as she sees me. She's prettier than her selfie, so much so I'm wondering why she had submitted an image so rushed, so random. She's slight and slender, very long limbs for a tiny person.

She slowly approaches me like a cougar stalking her prey. Sometimes new-time clients are like this, shocked and cautious.

She then takes one of her long fingernails, expertly manicured and embellished with shiny baubles, and pokes the side of my stomach with it.

"Yes," I say, "it's really me. Jim."

She then falls to her knees and begins to cry, a few stray tears falling on Jim's shoes. Grief has set in quickly. I want to immediately grab her from her kneeling position and embrace her, but I have to stop the urge. That's on page twenty-three in our training handbook. "Don't touch your client when they cry for the first time. Consoling them will disturb the grieving process." It also probably means fewer grieving sessions and less money for the Western World.

After a few minutes, she finally stops and rises, wiping her wet cheeks with the backs of her hands. She looks so young and fragile. Childlike. "You know I love you," she says.

"I love you, too." It's easy for me to respond, especially to Felicity.

She leads me to the couch and we sit for a while in silence. She eventually lies down, her head in my lap as she hugs her slim, dark legs to her chest, as if she has returned to becoming a baby in her mother's belly. I feel my dick start to harden and I'm shocked at how my body is responding to Felicity. I try to think of anything—kittens, my dead mother, geometric equations—to get my erection down.

I'm hoping that Felicity doesn't notice. I check my phone

and see that an hour has almost expired. "You can talk to me about anything," I say to her.

She abruptly sits up and I think that I've angered her in some way. "Why would I want to talk to you?" she says and I think that I've blown it. A light by the door flashes, signaling our time is almost up.

She stands up, smooths her dress of any wrinkles and proceeds for the door.

My mind whirls, and I try to think of something meaningful to say. "Hey, next time wear that red dress from Vegas."

Felicity stops in her tracks and slowly turns. She smiles widely, almost looking clownish. "You're good," she says. "You're really good." And then she leaves the room.

I honestly think that will be the last time I see her. I can't imagine what she'll write on her evaluation of me. But the next morning, I receive my assignment for the day. FELICITY, it says on my phone. 9 a.m. to Noon. Meeting: Company Park.

I don't like meetings in the Company Park. Everything feels staged, as if we are in an amusement park. The grass is so perfect that it looks fake. But most of all, I hate being there with all those other couples from the Western World.

Like I see a forty-something man in a corner by the stream with an older woman probably double our size. She's impeccably groomed, her probably dyed blonde hair curled and styled to perfection. I think that she's either wearing false eyelashes or has eyelash extensions underneath her glasses. They are lying on a blanket and the man's hand rests on her hip. Based on their age difference, I think that the man is the grief surrogate, it could even be Dan, but you can't be a hundred-percent sure of these things.

Felicity and I sit at the base of the hill, where there's a little more privacy. She is wearing the red dress, and I understand why Jim had left a message for her to do so. It's low-cut and tight at the waist, then flaring out Marilyn Monroe style. Felicity has packed a picnic lunch, full of sandwiches with the crusts cut off, little hot dogs wrapped in croissants, lemonade and sparkling water.

"You've always liked to eat," Felicity says, watching me down my third pig in a blanket. I'm trying to expand my waistline to be an exact fit of Jim's belt.

"Only because you made it," I tell her and she looks at me funny.

"Why are you doing this kind of work?" she asks.

I'm thrown off by her question. Customers aren't supposed to inquire about the surrogate's personal life, and I figure that she must have skipped over that instruction in the handbook. Still I answer her.

"I was actually on my way to being a psychologist. I stumbled across Reunion Stations and shadowed a grief surrogate. They recruited me and it's been two years."

My family—the few of them that are still alive—actually believe that I did become a psychologist. But it's not hard to pretend. Both involve confidentiality and I'd never reveal the real names of my customers, even if I did know them. Plus grief surrogacy is not exactly legal; it's new enough that even our local authorities are unaware of it.

She puts her hand on my chest and my heart begins to beat even faster. "I can't believe that you are really here. There's so much to say."

I usually let the customer take the lead, but today I can't help but interject my own feelings. "I want to take the hurt away. Make you whole."

Felicity's face immediately sours and she sits upright in her red dress. "I've always been whole," she says angrily and spends the rest of the morning chewing the edges of the egg salad and cucumber sandwiches.

* * *

The next morning, I receive my assignment. NEW CLIENT, my phone says. 10 a.m.

After stripping down in the Changing Room, I sit in the Waiting Room, on edge. My right leg bounces up and down.

Have I offended Felicity? I wonder. Or perhaps she's over her grief.

The door from the Transformation Room opens and then Jim appears, a bit older. He has a few wrinkles and gray hair in his wig. When he walks forward, I recognize the movement.

"What's going on?" I say, rising.

"I get my turn with Felicity." It's Dan's voice but then he adjusts it to a more Jim-like tenor. "I'm the Jim of the future."

"She didn't tell me that she wanted older."

"You sound like a lovesick boy. Christ. Be professional, man."

Professional, that's a laugh.

"Wish me luck, huh?" he saunters out and I feel sick to my stomach.

A number flashes—and I know it's now my turn.

My new customer is old, in her late seventies. Her husband died of stomach cancer about three months ago and she still obviously carries much guilt about it. I'm dressed in clothing from the 1960s, a skinny tie and beautiful sports coat that smells like mothballs.

When she walks in the Reunion Room and sees me, she immediately bursts in tears.

She apologizes over and over for every wrong she committed when they first got married. She didn't give him enough respect, she accused him of having affairs with his secretaries, told him that he was a lousy father.

She ends the session by saying, "Forgive me, please. If I could take it back, I would."

* * *

I have two more first-time reunions that day and one follow-up.

But my head's not in it. I'm wondering about Felicity. The next morning, even though I don't have to report to work until ten o'clock, I show up early, around eight.

Dan strolls in with his phone around nine, a towel tucked in around his middle. He crosses his legs in his chair. "Felicity is sure something special," he says to me. "Can't wait to get her in the sack soon."

The light flashes. "Oh, that's me." Dan walks towards the door to the Transformation Room. "Have a great day."

Why has Felicity chosen Dan to be her surrogate again? Dan doesn't even bother to do a proper voice impersonation. Perhaps she prefers an older Jim to imagine their lost future together.

My number eventually flashes and I enter the Transformation Room. I get Ms. Lillie while two chairs down Martin is putting the last touches on Dan. "An all-day date in the Honeymoon Suite, huh?" Martin says, putting some gray on the temples of Dan's wig and even adds a few strands of gray hair onto his bare chest.

They high-five each other and I feel more sick to my stomach. I don't understand. If Felicity wants to recreate their honeymoon, she should do it with me, a man in his thirties. I've only been assigned to the suite about six times. We are usually prescribed Viagra, and I see Martin give Dan a packet of pills.

The Honeymoon Suite is located on the penthouse level of the building and requires use of a special elevator located on the seventh floor. After I complete my three appointments, I go to the seventh floor and wait on a bench in the hallway. I'm maskless and in my street clothes. When the elevator dings, I immediately press the down button. The door opens to the seventh and a few people get out, including Felicity, the very last person. Another elevator going down to the first floor dings and we gather in front of its closed doors.

Felicity is standing next to me, but she doesn't know who I am. Her cheeks are flushed, her hair tousled. She's carrying an overnight bag. She's wearing a tropical-print sarong and I think I've never seen a more beautiful creature.

Once we are released onto the first floor, I make sure that I walk some distance behind her. She gets on a bus on the driver's side and I enter from the back side. I keep my eye focused on her face. She seems sated and jealousy burns inside me.

She gets out about nine stops down and I again follow. It's one of those hip commercial residential neighborhoods with quaint coffeehouses and charming restaurants. She goes into the walkway of the restored brick apartment buildings and types in her security code on a pad near an intercom.

I buy some flowers at a store across the street. I look at the names on the keypad. They are all last names and I have no idea which one represents the household of Jim and Felicity.

An older woman wearing an apron is sweeping the inside hallway and I rap the glass door for her to let me in. She looks at me suspiciously as she opens the door.

"Hi, I'm an old friend of Jim's. I wanted to give this to his widow. I just heard about his accident."

The woman takes the flowers from me. "I'll make sure that she gets this. But I can't let you in." She closes the door, leaving me outside. By the time I've reached the sidewalk, she calls after me. "Hey, who are you, by the way?" I continue walking as if I don't hear her.

The next morning I get my work message. I'm assigned to Felicity in Reunion Room Three.

"I know that you came by my apartment yesterday. I saw you."

"How did you know it was me?"

"I know that you followed me from the elevator. And the"

way you walked. I recognized your walk."

"Why did you drop me? I thought that you liked me."

"You aren't anything like Jim."

"I can be him. Just tell me what to do."

"Please, this is not something you can fake. You need to capture his essence. Either you have it, or you don't."

"Did you hear about Dan?" Martin asks me the next morning.

I say nothing while I sit buck naked in his chair.

"He died last night. Hit and run."

"What?"

"Do you know that he had a family and two kids?"

I shake my head. I had no idea.

"He was running late and didn't have time to change out of his surrogate identity. He was crossing the street when some asshole plows him over and takes off. What a bloody mess. Ms. Lillie saw the whole thing."

Ms. Lillie, working on someone two chairs down, solemnly nods her head.

"Do they know who did it?"

"The car had no plates; probably stolen. The police think it had to be someone who knew him, someone who had a real grudge against him. Even Dan's wife is being questioned. Apparently he was the type to knock her around."

I can't perform to the best of my ability the rest of the day. I wonder if the police will finally discover the existence of the Western World. But most of all, I wonder about Felicity. Now Dan is gone, she's probably feeling that she's lost Jim all over again.

After my last appointment, I go to Felicity's apartment building. This time when I arrive, the same woman, perhaps the building manager, is outside, cleaning some dog poop from the walkway.

"Oh, it's you again," she says. "I suppose you want to see

Vanessa. Well, she's gone. Packed everything and left." She is wearing purple gloves and I can smell the bleach in her bucket. "I know Jim was your friend and all, but he wasn't a good man. To tell you the truth, I'm glad to be rid of him. I had to call the police on him so many times. Once Vanessa was beaten so bad that she almost lost her eyesight.

"After Jim died in that car accident, it was like Vanessa had a new lease on life. And when the life insurance came in, I guess she felt she could really start over again."

She finishes scrubbing and removes her gloves. I stand in silence this whole time.

"You know what's weird?" she finally says. "After Jim got killed in that accident, I thought that she would be relieved, but she was mad."

"Mad?"

"She told me that she was mad that she didn't get a chance to kill him herself."

A month later things have pretty much returned to normal here at the Western World. Dan had a proper funeral, which none of us were invited to. The police are still looking for the killer, but they have no firm leads. The news has reported that he lied to his family about his profession and no one has come forward to identify what kind of work he was involved in. Based on the mask he was wearing, the authorities think it might be related to acting or some other kind of performance-related field.

When I enter the Waiting Room today, I see that Dan has posthumously won grief surrogate of the month. In addition to his name, they have included a quote from one of his customers' evaluations:

He has something that my husband Jim had. I can't really describe it. But he is a perfect match.

—Felicity

BLACK FRIDAY
Steve Brewer

On the day of the latest stock market crash, twenty-two people plunged to their deaths from New York City skyscrapers. One of them was pushed.

His name was Fred Barnes. He was my friend.

I knew Fred would never kill himself. His mother hanged herself when he was nine years old, and he'd never fully recovered. Whenever he had a few drinks, Fred would inevitably steer the conversation to his mother's suicide.

"That was when I went bad," he would moan. "After she died, I had no adult supervision."

Growing up on the streets of Brooklyn, Fred had learned he couldn't trust people. Only thing you can rely on, according to him, is cold, hard cash. That was the other reason I didn't believe his Black Friday "suicide." The crashing stock market would've meant nothing to Fred. He earned his money the old-fashioned way—he stole it.

I knew, because we became millionaires on the same heist. We were half of a four-man crew that knocked over a casino near Lake Tahoe during a Sierra Nevada blizzard. We tied up security guards and pointed guns at cash-room employees, but Mother Nature did the rest. We made our escape through wintry forests, towing plastic-wrapped bales of money on sleds behind two snowmobiles. By the time the cops could make their way through the drifts, we were across the state line, where we loaded the money onto a truck and disappeared.

At the time, the newspapers called it "the perfect crime." Who am I to argue? Sometimes on a job, everything just clicks. We stole nearly five million dollars, and we got away clean. Once we settled the up-front expenses—lodging, the abandoned snowmobiles, the rental truck, the discarded guns—each member of the four-man crew walked away with a little over a million dollars. In cash.

We played it the right way, stashing the money, lying low. But soon we got word that the victimized casino was secretly owned by the West Coast mob, a fact we had carelessly overlooked during the planning stages. The mobsters wanted their money back, and they wanted to make an example of the robbers.

We ran, of course. What else could we do?

Fred went for the safety of numbers. He changed his last name to Bigelow and disappeared into the eight million people who call New York City home. The loot from the heist bought him the lifestyle he'd always dreamed of. He rented a luxury apartment overlooking Central Park. He devoted most of his days to exploring the city's cafes. Last I heard, he had a new girlfriend half his age.

I'd taken the opposite approach, fleeing to the far side of the world. I ended up in Australia, in the mountains near a town called Muswellbrook, where I became a partner in a gold-mining operation. The work was hot and dusty, but we did well enough, and after a few years I stopped looking over my shoulder for mob hitmen.

Distance and discretion meant Fred and I hadn't communicated much lately, and it took two weeks before I heard the news of his death.

I knew the caller was a cop before he identified himself. It was the way he said my name instead of saying hello. "Alan Webster?"

I should've hung up. The cop had a New York accent, which meant he likely was on the other side of the world, too far away to do me any immediate harm. No reason for me to talk to him, but I was curious.

"Yes?"

He identified himself as Detective Vincent Ramos of the New York Police Department, and he said he had bad news.

"I'm sorry to tell you this," he said, "but Fred Bigelow is dead."

"Who?"

"Fred Bigelow."

My heart hammered, but I managed to keep my voice calm as I said, "I don't know anyone by that name."

"You sure?"

"Have you got the right Alan Webster? I haven't been to New York in years."

"But you've got a phone, right? We're talking on it right now."

I said nothing. Felt like I'd walked into a trap.

He said Fred Bigelow had taken a swan dive out of his fourteenth-floor apartment on Black Friday. Ramos had been assigned to investigate the death, though it seemed a clear case of suicide.

"That doesn't explain why you're calling me."

"I was going through his phone," Ramos said, "checking for anything unusual, and this number in Australia came up a few times. I've been unable to locate Mr. Bigelow's family. I thought you might be related to him."

"I told you, I don't know anybody named Bigelow. Sorry."

I was moving my thumb toward the button that would cut off the call when Ramos fired another volley: "Oh, I see the problem. You must've known him as Fred Barnes."

I was glad the detective couldn't see my face. I managed to say, "Excuse me?"

"We ran his prints," Ramos said. "And it turns out the guy

has another name, Fred Barnes, and a criminal record. No warrants out for him. So why was he living under the name Bigelow?"

I had no choice, so I stuck with denial. I told him again that I didn't know Fred and didn't know anything about any phone calls to New York.

"Is there somebody else there who uses your phone?"

"No. I live alone."

"A girlfriend? Somebody who used to date Fred Barnes?"

"Sorry," I said. "I can't help you."

Before he could spring another verbal trap, I disconnected the call. I stood perfectly still for a minute, blind to my surroundings, thinking about Fred and mobsters and Lake Tahoe. Then I snapped out of it and called Qantas to book a flight to New York City.

If Fred hadn't killed himself, and I couldn't believe that he had, then somebody else had done the job for him. Which likely meant the mob had located him, seven years after the casino heist. Lucky timing for the killers, to have Black Friday as an excuse for Fred's fourteen-story plummet.

If Detective Ramos had managed to track me down through Fred, there was a good chance the mobsters were doing the same. And they wouldn't call first. They'd just show up in Muswellbrook, ruining everything I'd built. Better to meet them on their own turf.

I couldn't get a flight out of Sydney until the next day, so I drove into the city and spent hours on an anonymous computer at an internet café, trying to track down the other two men involved in the Lake Tahoe heist.

One was easy to turn up. Mitch Taubel was dead, and his drowning in one of the Finger Lakes made a few headlines. The coroner ruled the death accidental, but I knew better. Mitch hated the great outdoors. If he was upstate, he'd been hiding there. And swimming in a chilly lake? Not a chance. If he died with water in his lungs, like the news accounts said, then somebody had been holding his head under.

The fourth member of our crew? I couldn't find him, which was even more troubling.

Davis Carr had vanished a year ago. At least, I couldn't find any trace of him since then, anywhere on the internet. Using a throwaway phone, I risked calls to old mates in New York, L.A. and Chicago, asking after Davis, and nobody could remember hearing what happened to him. He'd simply disappeared. The house where he'd been living in California was boarded up, the swimming pool drained and collecting leaves.

Two possibilities there. One, Davis heard the mobsters were on his trail, and he went underground. Or, two, they found him and *put* him underground. Either way, Davis Carr was no help to me.

That left only me from the Lake Tahoe heist crew. I'd been the youngest of the four, the one who did the heavy lifting, the one who'd run the farthest. I had to assume the mob knew my name by now.

I could've gone into hiding. Just driven my Land Rover into the outback and kept going, out to where the arid landscape is fit only for kangaroos. Sit around barefoot, waiting for a hitman to find me. But that wasn't the way I wanted to spend my days.

Better to run right at the danger. Find the mook responsible for Fred's death and make an example of him. That wouldn't necessarily solve the problem. The mob would send another guy and another guy. Always plenty of cannon fodder among the young men trying to make their bones. But if I took out a few, they would eventually get the point. And if one of the guidos got lucky and put me down first? At least I would be done with it. I wouldn't be looking over my shoulder for the rest of my life.

* * *

I had lots of time to mull it over during the twenty-two-hour flight to New York. Even in first class, the jet felt cramped to a lanky guy who is accustomed to wide-open spaces. My claustrophobia wasn't helped by the flight attendant, a perky brunette who fluttered around me like a butterfly.

At customs, a uniformed officer asked me lots of questions, so many that I began to fear that I'd been flagged by the FBI or Homeland Security. But eventually the officer waved me through, and I scooted out of JFK's Terminal 8.

New York was cold and damp, just the opposite of where I live, and the chill went to my bones as I flagged down a cab. I wore a battered leather duster, the only coat I owned these days. Protection enough from the ceaseless Australian wind, but not warm enough for real winter.

The cabbie had the heat turned up. He was a Russian immigrant with a huge gray mustache and a twinkle in his eye. It took only a few carefully phrased questions before we veered off to Brooklyn to see his cousin Ivan, who just so happened to be selling a pistol. Six hundred dollars, cash only. Everybody wanted cash since the stock market crash; they feared the banks and credit card companies would go next.

The gun turned out to be an aged revolver, a Colt with a six-inch barrel. Cousin Ivan wanted twice what the gun was worth, but I peeled off the bills without hesitation. Worth it to me to avoid a lot of messy paperwork.

An hour later, I reached midtown Manhattan, wearing my outlaw coat, my loaded six-shooter stuck in my belt. All I needed was a cowboy hat. Nobody gave me a second look as I checked into the Winchester Hotel. Guess they see all kinds there.

It didn't take long to unpack my carry-on bag. I'd only brought one change of clothes and the usual toiletries. The bed beckoned after the long flight, but it was mid-afternoon. If I slept now, I'd be up all night and the jet lag would be even worse. Instead, I used my phone to search up the nearest clothing shop for "big and tall" men. Only six blocks away. I could manage that, even in the icy wind.

I shaved and took a shower and put on my fresh shirt. I buttoned the duster up to my chin and went shopping. I came away with layers: flannel shirts and sweaters and a wool sport coat and—in a splurge that was unusual for me—a black cashmere overcoat. It cost seven hundred bucks, but it fit like a dream and I couldn't pass it up. An eager clerk bagged my purchases and rolled up my leather duster into a bag of its own. I felt less like an outsider, walking along the crowded sidewalk in the warm overcoat. And there was room in its deep inside pocket for the Colt.

I visited a bank on the way back to my hotel and withdrew four thousand dollars from one of my Australian accounts, all in hundred-dollar bills. You need lots of tip money in New York.

I stopped occasionally on the sidewalk, stepping out of the traffic flow, pretending to check my phone or rearrange my packages. I couldn't see anybody tailing me, but it was only a matter of time.

Back in my hotel room, I had time to put away my new clothes before there was a knock on the door. I carried the cowboy gun with me as I checked the peephole. A man waited in the carpeted corridor for me to answer the door. He had droopy hound-dog eyes and thinning black hair and he wore a rumpled suit the color of mud. He held up a gold badge for me to see.

I stashed my unregistered revolver in my carry-on bag, then answered the door.

"Yes?"

"Alan Webster?"

I knew that voice. From the phone.

"Detective Vincent Ramos," the cop said. "You got a minute?"

"Do I have a choice?"

Ramos shrugged. He was eight inches shorter than me, but

his shoulders were broad and his hands were thick and scarred. He looked like he was used to getting his way.

I stepped aside. He came into the room, casually checking the bathroom and closet to make sure we were alone. The room came with a small sofa, and Ramos plopped down and made himself comfortable. I rolled a chair over from the desk and sat so we faced each other, a low coffee table between us.

"Didn't take you long to find out I was in town," I said.

"I had an alert on your passport, in case you decided to come home to the good old U.S. of A. And that's exactly what you did, though you claimed on the phone that you didn't know Fred Barnes."

"Maybe it's a coincidence," I said. "Maybe I was planning to come to New York anyway."

"You bought your ticket less than twenty-four hours before your flight."

"I'm an impulsive traveler."

"Ah." He nodded, like he was finally getting it. "I can wait. This is a comfortable couch. I'm on the clock whether I'm sitting here in this nice warm room or out pounding the pavement."

"I thought Fred Barnes committed suicide. That's what you said on the phone."

"That's how it looks," Ramos said. "We even have a witness."

I cocked an eyebrow at him.

"His girlfriend, Katy Redmond. She said Barnes was upset about the stock market and threw himself through the window."

"You believe her?"

"No reason not to," he said. "But I checked him out, doing the due diligence, you know, and he's got a fake name. And a record. And here's this phone number in Australia. And when I call it, the guy on the other end gets all squirrelly. Then he flies to New York right away."

I nodded.

"See my problem?" he said. "If you don't know Fred Barnes, then why does word of his death bring you halfway around the world?"

I'd worked on this answer during my flight to New York.

"I knew Fred, but as Barnes not Bigelow. That tripped me up at first, when you called, then I got nervous."

"Why?"

I paused, just as I'd rehearsed it in my head on the plane, then said, "Fred got himself into some dicey situations sometimes."

"Illegal situations?"

"I got the impression he had a lot of secrets."

Ramos nodded.

"What about you, Mr. Webster? I can't find any criminal record on you. You got secrets?"

"Everybody has secrets."

"Did you and Barnes ever work together?"

"Fred was just a guy I knew. We'd get together occasionally and have a few drinks. After I moved away, we kept in touch by phone, but it was very casual."

"He talk about his financial situation? What he did for a living?"

"Not really. We'd talk about baseball and the weather. He was always recommending some wine for me to try. He didn't seem to be hurting for money, but I never asked."

Ramos studied me for a moment, then said, "Would it surprise you to know he had a safe in his apartment? We had to get a locksmith to drill it open. It was stuffed with eighty thousand dollars in cash."

"His girlfriend didn't know the combination?"

"She claims she'd never even seen Fred open the box during the four months she'd known him. Which means that was 'extra' money, you know. Beyond what he needed to live day to day."

"An emergency fund. Not that unusual, though it is a lot of cash to keep on hand."

"You must not be hurting for money yourself," Ramos said. "A next-day flight to New York must've cost you a fortune."

"I don't worry about money, Detective. I literally own a gold mine."

"Must be nice."

"It is."

"Still, you drop everything and hop a plane to come check on your dead friend?"

"I thought I might be able to help in some way," I said, sounding hardly rehearsed at all. "I didn't know anything about his family, but there must be—"

"No family. Just the girlfriend."

"She must be devastated."

Ramos shrugged.

"Do you know how I can find her? Maybe I can help plan a memorial or something."

"She's still living in the same apartment," he said. "She spent the first couple nights in a hotel. But once the window was fixed, she moved back in. She said the place was already paid for. No sense letting it sit empty."

"Sentimental type, huh?"

"Let me put it this way," Ramos said. "When I was interviewing her? I made sure not to stand near the window.

Katy Redmond answered my knock by opening the door a crack and shouting past the chain latch: "If you're a bill collector, you're wasting your time."

"I'm not a bill collector."

"The guy who held the lease here is *dead*," she continued, as if I'd said nothing. "So whatever he owed you people, you're out of luck."

"I'm still not a bill collector."

She squinted at me through the gap. "Then who are you?"

"I was a friend of Fred's. I heard about his death and I

thought I'd see if there's anything I could do to help."

"Took you long enough," she said. "He's been dead two weeks."

"I just got the news. I live in Australia."

Her dark eyes widened. I couldn't see much of her through the gap, but she seemed to be in her late twenties, trim and fit. She wore a ponytail and a purple leotard.

"Did I catch you during your workout?" I said. "Is this a bad time?"

"I was rehearsing. Modern dance. Hang on."

She closed the door. After a minute, I heard her unlatch the chain, then the door opened. She wore a shimmery black robe over her workout clothes. It covered her to her knees, but still seemed a flimsy garment for greeting strangers. I waited until she gestured me inside before I crossed the threshold.

"I'm Alan Webster. I knew Fred for nearly twenty years."

We shook hands.

"Katy. I knew him about twenty minutes."

I followed her into the apartment, which was decorated with designer prints and low, modern furniture that looked uncomfortable. Kitchen to the left of the entry, bathroom to the right, both empty. The living area was dominated by a wall of windows, which drew me across the room. They looked out over the winter-bare trees of Central Park and a slice of sky churning with gray clouds. The windows were three large panes, reaching from knee-high to the ceiling. The center pane looked cleaner than the others.

"It's thick glass," she said. "You wouldn't think it would break so easily."

At minimum, I thought, it would take a running start. Even a big guy like Fred would've needed a lot of momentum to throw himself through that glass.

"Must've been difficult for you," I said. "Seeing him die like that."

"It happened so fast, I could barely process it. Next thing I knew, the apartment was full of cops."

I turned away from the windows and sat in a hard chair that faced the sofa where she'd curled up, her bare feet tucked under her.

"Had Fred been depressed?"

"The stock market thing hit him hard. It was like the last straw, you know? The whole country's going to hell, and now the economy's going, too."

"Is that what he said?"

"You mean, before he jumped?"

I nodded somberly.

"No, he didn't say anything. He just ran across the room and threw himself against the window, like a bird. The glass gave way, and out he went."

"It's a long way down."

"Yes, it is."

"I suppose he had time to reconsider, as he was falling."

She frowned. "Are you trying to make me feel bad? Is that why you're here? Because I got enough of that from the cops."

"Sorry. I sometimes make the mistake of saying out loud thoughts that would be better kept to myself. It's a hazard of spending a lot of time alone."

"Talking to yourself?"

"Having lots of thoughts."

She smiled, but it was unsteady, as if she'd fallen out of practice. "What are you thinking about now?"

"I was wondering how you and Fred met."

"He came to a theater where I was dancing."

"That doesn't sound like Fred."

"A friend brought him. We went out for drinks after the show, and next thing you know, I'm moving in. Fred took care of everything, bought me anything I wanted, gave me the freedom to pursue my career. Now the bills are coming due, and I don't even have a checkbook of my own."

"What are you going to do at the end of the month, when

the rent comes due?"

"Move out," she said. "And, before you ask, no, I don't know where I'm going. I'm broke."

"The police told me they found eighty thousand dollars in a safe here."

"Which they promptly confiscated," she said bitterly. "Said it was 'evidence.' Evidence of what? The man jumped out a window."

I waited a beat, then said, "Did Fred ever mention why he kept so much money on hand?"

"I didn't even know it was there."

"How did he pay for things? When you when out to eat, did he pay cash?"

"He used a card like everyone else in this century. What are you getting at?"

"Just trying to understand," I said. "Even if he lost a lot of money in the stock market, he still had his emergency fund. What could be so bad that he'd kill himself?"

"I don't know." Her gaze went steely. "You'd have to ask Fred."

I slept for ten hours, awakening to a new day in New York City, and I felt revived. I threw open the drapes to let in the morning sunshine, and put on the white terry-cloth robe that came with the hotel room. It barely reached my knees, though the label claimed that one size fits all. Without bothering with the menu, I called room service and ordered an entire pot of coffee, along with toast and scrambled eggs and bacon. An American breakfast. One of the things they do right in this country.

I brushed my teeth and washed up, then went back to the window, which overlooked Fifth Avenue. The sidewalks already teemed with people, and street traffic was at a stand-still. More people in a single block than the entire population of Muswellbrook.

Two sharp raps on my door. A deep voice in the hall said, "Room service."

I went to the peephole in the door and looked out. A room-service waiter stood in the hall with a rolling cart covered in dishes. He had a long, apelike face, which was exaggerated by his receding hairline. His standard-issue green jacket was too tight, and the sleeves barely reached his wrists, so he made me think of an organ grinder's monkey. As I watched, he looked up and down the empty hall. Something furtive about that look.

I got the cowboy gun out of my bag and held it behind my back as I opened the door in my robe. I gave Ape Face a big smile and asked him to roll the cart over to the window. He frowned, but he slowly pushed the cart across the room.

I was watching his hands, so I was ready when he flipped a cloth napkin aside and reached for a little pistol hidden beneath it. I took a long step forward and stuck the barrel of the Colt in his big ear and cocked back the hammer.

"If you make a mistake, your brains will be all over this room. Do you understand?"

He nodded, wincing against the gun barrel in his ear.

With my free hand, I took the little pistol away from him. I slipped it into the pocket of my too-short robe. Ape Face stood very still, the revolver in his ear.

"All right," I said. "I'm gonna ask you a few questions. If I like the answers, maybe I let you walk out of here."

He looked sidelong at me, a flicker of hope in his hooded eyes.

"What's your name?"

"George."

"Who sent you here, George?"

"Nobody," George said. "I mean, nobody you know. A local guy hired me, a broker."

"And this broker," I said, "who is his client?"

"I don't know—"

"Is it the West Coast mob?"

George froze. After a few seconds, he nodded.

"So, they know I'm back on American soil. That didn't take long."

"I don't know anything about that," George said. "I got a phone call, that's all. They told me to come here."

"And what were you supposed to do after you killed me, George? Were you supposed to call someone?"

Another nod.

"Okay, George, here's how it's going to go. You're gonna walk out that door and you're gonna call that number and tell them what happened here. Tell them that the next goon they send gets a bullet in the brain. You got that?"

George carefully nodded.

I stepped away from him and said, "Go tell 'em."

He suddenly wheeled toward me, swinging one of his long arms at my head. I ducked away from the blow and punched him in the ribs, hard enough that the air whoofed out him. Still, he lunged at me, trying to bull me over. I sidestepped him, neatly as a matador, and cracked him across the brow with the barrel of the Colt.

George grunted and cradled his head in both hands. Once he caught his breath, he mumbled, "I had to try it."

"Sure you did, George. And I had to stop you. The only reason I didn't shoot you was I didn't want to mess up this hotel room. Don't bleed on the carpet."

George checked his hands, but there was no blood. Just a purpling bruise above his eye.

"Go tell 'em," I said. "I'll be right here. Maybe they'll send somebody smarter next time."

George snarled at me, but I waved the big pistol at him and it shooed him out. I waited a few minutes to make sure he didn't come back and kick in the door, then I went to the room-service cart. The food had gone cold, but the coffee was still hot.

I stood at the window, sipping coffee, waiting for my heartbeat to return to normal, the pockets of my robe weighed down with guns.

I didn't stay in that hotel room, of course. I may be bold, but I'm not an idiot. Once George reported what I'd said, they'd send a battalion of goons to the Winchester Hotel.

I got dressed, packed my bag and left the hotel without checking out. I caught a cab and told the driver the one address in Manhattan I knew by heart.

Ten minutes later, I climbed out into sunshine around the corner from where Fred Barnes had met his end. I carried my bag around to the front of the building, the Colt in my inside pocket, George's little flat pistol in my side pocket, clutched in my right hand. I didn't expect trouble here, but I was ready.

The rotund doorman remembered my bribe from the day before and beamed at me as he held open the door to Katy Redmond's building. I tucked a hundred-dollar bill in the breast pocket of his coat. Keeping the wheels greased. No better social lubricant than money.

Perhaps money was what I needed to get Katy tell me the truth about Fred's death. If I started peeling hundreds off a roll, it wouldn't take long to find her price. She was desperate for start-over money.

After I stepped off the elevator onto the fourteenth floor, I checked doors until I found a closet used by the janitor. I tucked my bag among the brooms and buckets. I didn't want to show up at Katy's door with bag in hand, like I was trying to take Fred's place.

I knocked with my left hand, my right keeping the little pistol warm in my pocket. After a minute, the door opened an inch and Katy Redmond peeked past the chain.

"Back so soon?"

"Good morning to you, too," I said. "I've got more questions."

She glanced over her shoulder. "It's not a good time."

"You've got company?"

"No, it's just that—"

"Step back."

"What?"

I shouldered through the door, the latch chain snapping with a "ping!" Katy managed to jump back out of the way, nimble on her dancer's feet, and the door missed her by inches.

"What are you *doing*? You can't just bust in here—"

"Sure I can," I said. "I just did."

She glowered at me, her face so red it nearly matched her fleece bathrobe. This one was floor-length and a lot more modest than the one she'd donned for me the day before. Her dark hair was loose around her shoulders, and her face was scrubbed clean of makeup.

The apartment wasn't as tidy as it had been, either. Clothes were strewn across the living room furniture, and a pizza box decorated the coffee table. Most notable was the kitchen counter, where two red coffee cups sat, both of them still steaming.

I pulled the little pistol out of my pocket and showed it to her.

Her eyes cut toward the bedroom, an involuntary twitch that gave her away.

"Back up," I said.

She backed across the living room until she was clear of the door that led into the apartment's one bedroom. The door stood open a few inches.

"Come on out," I called. "Come out of the bedroom or I'll shoot her."

Katy let out a little yip of concern, but I ignored her. My eyes were on the bedroom door. I held the pistol close to my body, finger on the trigger, waiting.

After a tense minute, the bedroom door swung open the rest of the way, and a heavily-muscled man stepped through the doorway. He wore gray sweatpants and a disarming smile, but no shirt or shoes. He held out his hands to show he was unarmed.

His hair had turned gray since I'd seen him last, but I recognized him right away.

"Hello, Davis," I said. "Funny seeing you here."

Davis Carr shrugged, still grinning, as if he could charm his way out of this situation. Not this time.

"Let me guess," I said. "You were the friend who took Fred to see Katy dance."

He nodded.

"And you made sure they met afterward."

Another nod.

"Why were you screwing around in Fred's life? Were you planning to rip him off?"

"Not exactly. But I do have a lot of debts, now that you mention it, and I figured Fred would have access to some cash."

"How are you broke?" I said. "You had a million dollars."

"A million doesn't go as far as it used to," Davis said. "I made a few bad investments. Developed some bad habits."

He touched a finger to his nose.

"Next thing you know, I'm scrambling around, trying to keep loan sharks off my neck. It was crazy."

"And you thought of Fred."

"He was the only one who kept in touch," Davis said. "I never heard anything from Mitch, and you'd fucked off to Australia. I needed help. What was I supposed to do?"

"So you recruited Katy."

"It wasn't like that," he said. "Not exactly. But you know how Fred was. He had a weakness for younger women with dark hair."

"They reminded him of his mother."

"Whatever, dude. I saw an opportunity."

I glanced over at Katy. She'd moved away from us, toward the kitchen, and stood with her arms crossed, glaring at Davis Carr.

"Sorry, honey," I said. "You probably thought you'd found true love. But this guy's not capable of such feelings."

"Hey, man," Davis said. "That's harsh."

"You used her. And when Fred found out, you threw him through that window over there."

The smile slipped back onto Davis' face. "The cops ruled it a suicide."

"I never believed it," I said. "That glass is too thick. Nobody could run hard enough to bust through it."

"Sure you could," he said.

"Try it."

"What?"

"Run across the room and throw yourself against that window," I said. "Just as hard as you can."

"You're crazy."

"Come on. Prove your point. If it breaks, you're right."

"And I'm dead."

"Maybe it'll hold. But if you don't run at it, and I mean right now, you're dead for sure."

I raised the pistol so it pointed right at his face.

Davis wasn't smiling now. His eyes cut from the pistol to the window and back again.

"Run, Davis. Run right at that window. If it doesn't break, I'll let you go."

"You're fucking with me."

"Last chance."

My finger tightened on the trigger.

"Fuck it," Davis said.

He turned and ran toward the glass, his bare feet silent on the carpet. Just as he reached the window, he pulled up, so he wouldn't hit it full force. As I'd known he would.

The little pistol snapped in my hand, and its .22-caliber bullet raced across the room and hit the window just as Davis threw his shoulder against the glass. The shattered glass hung there half a second, Davis splayed against it, then it all went tumbling out of sight.

Cold air whooshed into the apartment. Fourteen floors below, horns honked and people screamed.

Sirens howled outside by the time I reached Detective Vincent Ramos on the phone.

"What have you got, Webster?"

"Fred Barnes didn't commit suicide. A guy named Davis Carr hurled him through that window."

"But the girlfriend said—"

"Katy lied."

I looked across the room at Katy. Her eyes were flooded with tears and pleading.

"She and Davis were setting Fred up to take his money. I came to her place and found them both here. Davis admitted what he'd done. Then he jumped out that same window."

"He *what*?"

"He must've felt terribly guilty," I said. "To kill himself that way."

"You're shitting me."

"Come see for yourself."

I pocketed the phone, then turned toward the door.

"You're leaving me here?" Katy cried. "For the police?"

"Time to face the music, sweetheart."

"They'll put me in jail!"

"You can always go out the window instead. Just like Fred."

I didn't wait around to see which she chose.

HEY NINETEEN
W.H. Cameron

Because the universe hates me, Quince Kinsrow is waiting when I turn in to the parking lot at the Downhill Motor Lodge. Even inside a parka the size of a rain barrel, there's no missing his bandy legs or the careless way he flicks his cigarette into the snow. The old scarecrow has been retired three months, yet he still shows up uninvited to random call-outs—to "mentor" me.

As if hauling the dead requires a goddamn thesis advisor.

"What took you so long, little girl?" he says once I park the Stiff and step out into needle-sharp sleet. "I'm freezing my nubbins off."

On a clear day I can make the eleven winding miles from the Old Mortuary to the high country hamlet of Crestview in twenty minutes. On an icy November night, I'm lucky I made it at all. According to the brochure, this mountain hamlet is Barlow County's gateway to the high-country splendor of Lost Brother Butte—hiking and camping in summer, skiing and snowshoeing in winter. According to anyone who's actually been here, Crestview is the shabby home of one nursing home, two dive bars, and three seedy motels—with the Downhill taking the prize for Most Squalid.

"Feel free to fuck off, Quince."

A wet burble spills from the gash he uses for a mouth. A

laugh, maybe. Or a symptom of emphysema. Deep into his seventies, he's long-limbed and hunger-strike-thin—the latter a product of his two-pack-a-day Pall Mall habit. Yet somehow he manages to have the energy of a teen meth addict.

I push past him into the motel office and stomp the slush from my boots. Behind the high counter, the clerk looks up from his cellphone. His green irises swim in a sea of red— because of the over-amped fluorescents or the half-eaten brownie on the desk I don't want to know. The name tag pinned haphazardly to his grease-spotted cardigan reads GERT. First or last name, I'm not sure.

"Did you call the body in?"

"Musta been…" He blinks, then stands slowly like it's a skill he's still mastering. "Uh, yeah. Musta been someone else." He frowns and his eyes drop to the mess at my feet. As if the carpet has been cleaned this millennium.

"Have you seen the EMTs?"

"They bailed. Said I should expect a doctor." He blinks again, then reaches up and gives his long white ponytail a tug. "Are you the doctor?"

"I'm mortuary transport."

"A girl?"

Quince sidles up beside me, his breath an aromatherapy nightmare of stale tobacco and last month's tuna melt.

"I'm her supervisor."

I need every last shred of restraint not to chuck him through the front window. Instead, I scan the motel parking lot. Based on the number of cars and SUVs piling up with snow, the place is barely a quarter full. No sign of the medical examiner's Escalade, which puts me in limbo. Fire and Rescue should have hooked the body up to a wireless EKG so the doctor could pronounce remotely. I guess they had more important things to do. On a night like this, even in sparsely populated Barlow County, there's probably accidents from Trout Rot to Handbrake.

I dig under layers of fleece and nylon for my phone. My call to the doctor goes straight to voice mail. I reach the county dispatcher, but she puts me on hold before I can ask about Varney's ETA.

"Shit." I disconnect.

Hopefully he's on his way. Hopefully he's not flipped over in a ditch.

I turn to Gert. "When the doctor arrives, tell him I'm waiting next door." Their coffee sucks, but the East Slope Mercantile lacks the Downhill's faint, ammonia-tamped whiff of urine.

"Melisende—" Quince drapes a too-familiar hand over my shoulder, "—don'tcha think we need to look in on the decedent?"

I twist out of his grasp. "*We* don't need to do anything. This isn't *your* job anymore."

"Someone's gotta keep an eye on you."

The one good thing about Quince is his needling quiets the doubtful voice in my own head. Only seven months earlier my husband left me broke and homeless and out of options. The last thing I expected was for his aunt and uncle to offer me a home and a job.

I'm still learning, but the basics are easy enough. Zip the body into a bag, strap it to a cot, roll it out to the Stiff—the fusty van that serves as first-call vehicle for Bouton Funerary Service. Depending on the circumstances, I'll transport the remains to the hospital morgue or to the funeral home. Usually it's someone whose death was not unexpected, the old or infirm. But because Bouton has the county contract to handle medical examiner removals, I may be called to vehicle collisions, hunting accidents, drownings—even the occasional wrongful death.

No such luck tonight, a probable stroke or heart attack according to the call-out. Means we don't get to rubberneck a dead man.

"Quince—" I give him a hard shove toward the door. "Go.

Home."

Taking a hint—even delivered in the imperative—isn't part of his skillset. "Darling, I've been doing this since before you first latched onto your mama's teat. Based on my deep well of experience, I say we don't know when the doc'll get here so it's our job to assess the situation."

He's utterly full of shit. He's also utterly relentless. I sigh and turn back to the clerk. "What's the room number?"

"Uh, twenty-four?"

"You sure?"

Lacking the wits to blush, he manages a hesitant nod.

"Is the room locked?"

Another nod.

"Great. I'll hold the key till the medical examiner arrives." I throw a glare at Quince. "There, the situation is assessed."

"Who you think's in charge here, little girl?" he says, beckoning with a brown claw.

Wayward eyes on me, Gert hands the room key to Quince. I snatch at it and miss as he lopes out into the bitter night. All I can do is follow at a trot, swearing at his jangly back.

The motel is laid out in two wings with the doors all facing the parking lot. The decedent's room is at the end nearest the Mercantile. Thready light bleeds through the curtained window beside the door. At least two sets of boot prints are sharp in the snow blown against the threshold. The EMTs haven't been gone long.

"Quince, for the last time—"

"The boys probably left paperwork inside."

Doubtful, but then they shouldn't have left the body unattended either. "Even if they did, it's not for us." My nettled brain spits up a line of policy. *Mortuary transport acts under the direction and authority of the deputy medical examiner or law enforcement.*

He blows air dismissively, then throws open the door.

The room is dominated by a queen-sized bed and a wide-screen TV on the wall opposite. A mini fridge, chipped dresser, and two bedside tables complete the spartan furnishings. A framed print over the bed might be titled *Bob Ross The Scream*. The light from the overhead fixture seems to die in the jaundiced walls and thin, stained carpeting, but the porn flick paused on the TV casts a harsh pall across the naked man lying at the foot of the bed.

His feet are on the floor, with one hand out-flung and the other at his groin. Lips drawn back from clenched teeth. But the showstopper is the distended phallus. I've read about postmortem priapism, the death erection, in the mortuary science books we keep in the break room. I could have gone my whole life without seeing it in the engorged flesh.

Quince emits a long, rattling exhalation. "He hadn't oughta gone out like that." Wheezing, he blunders across the threshold, arms outstretched like a Boris Karloff cosplayer.

I give his parka a hard yank. "Are you out of your mind?" Quince may be a death call tourist, but I need this job. "We can't go in there."

"Did those pudknockers even *try* to revivitate him?"

If this is how the EMTs found the body, there wouldn't have been anything to revive. The skin is waxy and ashen, the lower legs purple with pooling blood—indicators of my two favorite mortises: pallor and livor. It's probably too soon for rigor, but not by much. He's been dead a good two or three hours.

I give the room a quick scan. Cellphone on the bedside table with the TV remote, room phone on the mini fridge next to the electric kettle. Jeans and a khaki expedition shirt spill from a leather duffel on the floor beside the dresser. Socks, underwear, and a pair of ankle boots in the corner. No other personal items are in evidence, though I can't see into the bathroom. The closet is an exposed recess with a single wire hanger on a wooden dowel.

As for the man himself, he's in Quince's demographic, with

short grey hair and crevasses eroding his face and neck. Wiry hair forests his thin chest. White foam has crusted at the corners of his mouth.

I pull Quince back through the doorway. "We need to get out of here."

"Let me at least spread a sheet over him."

"No. We don't touch anything."

"Why the hell not?"

Because of the white foam and clenched jaw. Because the curtains are closed, and both phones are beyond the man's reach. I draw a frigid breath.

"Because this might be a crime scene."

That's when the lights go out.

It's not just the dead man's room. All of Crestview falls into sudden darkness. My first instinct is to feel for the door and pull it shut. I expect an argument, but Quince only coughs up a despondent whine as I grab the key from the doorknob and pocket it.

Up toward the lobby, one of the motel room doors opens and someone shouts, "The fuck? My phone only has one percent."

"This happen a lot?" I say to Quince.

"Welcome to your first Barlow County winter."

I pull out my own phone. The battery icon is solid. I try the doctor, get voice mail again. As least the county dispatcher doesn't put me on hold. After I explain the situation, she says, "Fire and Rescue should have reported this, but it's been crazy since the storm hit. Is the scene secure?"

"Locked up tight."

"I'll alert the sheriff. But we've got wrecks in Antiko, a domestic out at Dryer Lake, and a fire all the way up to Pilchik. It's all hands on deck, so I have no idea when someone will be there."

Barlow County isn't on anyone's Top Ten list. We're not the biggest, not the smallest. Our landscape is pretty but not beautiful, scenic but not breathtaking. People ski our half-assed mountain because it's cheaper and less crowded than Mount Hood or Mount Bachelor. Even our golf resort, an unexpected greensward carved out of the high desert, exists only for those who don't want to pay the fees at resorts near Bend or in Sun Valley. As a result, our Sheriff's Department can barely field a softball team. Fire and Rescue is ninety percent volunteers—none cops. Our crime scene tech teaches high school science. Even Dr. Varney is a family physician first, medical examiner second.

It could be a long night.

Off in the darkness, a motor rumbles to life. "You coming?" His face red in the sudden flare of a cigarette, Quince heads toward the sound.

"Where are you going?"

"BRR has a generator."

A pale purple light flickers to life beyond the Mercantile.

My choice seems to be between hanging with Quince in a shitkicker bar or waiting for the cavalry in the Stiff. Tough call, but as the wind kicks up and snow pelts my face, I sigh and trudge after him.

The dive's name came about due to a mistake. Rather than demand the neon sign be fixed, the owner accepted the fuck-up at a steep discount and hung it over the door. Apropos, if you ask me. With its corrugated metal walls and unfinished concrete floor, BRR has all the character of a pole barn. The galvanized steel bar is topped by puce Formica and bookended by cold cases filled with party-packs of Busch and Natty Light. Mismatched booths line the walls. Tables are scattered haphazardly under shop lights. At the far end, duct tape frames a dance area next to the sagging plywood stage. On the walls, posters of boobsome women peddle guns, ammo, and fishing gear. A matched pair of mounted mule deer heads are already hung with Christmas lights, two weeks before Thanksgiving.

Quince shrugs out of his parka and makes for the bar. A number of the more ambulatory residents from across the road at Crestview Assisted Living are already there. They all quickly fall into hail-fellow-well-met back slaps. Quince's people, I guess. Other oldsters are spread throughout the cavernous space, recent comers distinguished by the snow melting on their coats and balding pates. A jazz guitar tune, like something from my grandmother's vinyl record collection, competes with the geezer gab in a kind of feedback loop that soon will have everyone shouting to be heard.

I'm about to say "fuck it" when I spot a young woman swaying in front of the jukebox. In magenta jeans and a yellow T-shirt made for someone who shops in the back-to-school department, she looks as out of place as I feel. A couple of the old men have noticed her too. If I was tempted to wait in the Stiff, their predatory focus changes my mind. Old dogs can still bite.

Almost as if she senses my gaze, she rotates my way. Her broad face is framed by a blunt-cut blond bob, her eyes are over-sized and stormy blue. Her lipstick matches her pants. From behind, I placed her around my age—mid-twenties. But her round cheeks and those startling eyes push my estimate into her teens, despite the longneck Corona in one hand. Fake ID or an indifferent BRR-tender, take your pick.

Unblinking, she scans me head to toe, then tosses me a half-smile before turning back to the jukebox. Maybe she's looking for something recorded in her lifetime.

Out of inertia, I move toward Quince at the bar. The spirited discussion he's having with his clot of fogeys pulls my attention away from the girl.

"—saw him at the Fillmore in what, sixty-eight or nine." Quince's voice is thick with nostalgic pride.

"Wasn't he that game show guy?"

Quince hisses disdainfully. "That was later, mid-eighties—"

"I remember him on *Hollywood Squares*. Or maybe the *Pyramid* one. Guy was hilarious."

"Sure, sure," Quince grumbles. "But before *that*, he was the real fuckin' deal. I mean, he mostly did session or tour band work, but the guy performed with just about everyone at one time or another. Clapton, Beck, Steely Dan, Buffalo Springfield. He could play *anything*—"

"Quince." I give his arm a tug.

When he turns, his face is full of color. "What's wrong, girl? Forget your wallet?"

I feel my lips compress. "Who are you talking about?"

His face goes carefully blank. "Have a drink. Loosen up."

His own glass holds a double shot of something temptingly golden. But unlike him, I still have a body to deal with. "You and I need to have a conversation."

I wave the BRR-tender over. "Aren't you that girl who drives the corpse wagon?" he says as he fills a glass with Diet Coke.

I pay for my drink without dignifying that with a response. Quince pouts as I drag him to an empty booth against the back wall. I drop my coat on the bench as a power ballad kicks in, something else from my grandmother's collection. The girl hasn't left the jukebox.

When the song ends, I lean across the table. "Tell me about the dead guy."

He drains his glass in one swallow. "You ready for another?"

I glance at my untouched Diet Coke. "You knew who he was before I even got here."

"What makes you think that?"

"The goddamn ants in your pants. The fact you couldn't wait to get through that door. And look at you now, mooning like your old hound dog died."

"Never had a dog." He manages to exhale the dregs of his last cigarette. "We shoulda covered him up, turned off that damn movie."

"The EMTs left things as-is for a reason."

"You're talking out of yer ass."

"I'm making sure we don't fuck up the scene." Quince can't possibly understand. He's lived in Barlow County his whole life. I'm the weird outsider who drives the corpse wagon. If he compromises the scene, well that's just kooky old Quince for ya. If I do... "Unlike you, I actually *need* this job."

"All I know is it isn't right."

"Who is he, anyway?"

"Damn, girl, you kidding me?"

I hate it when he calls me girl. "Quince—"

"He's *Kenny Bing.*" He intones the name like he's reading from scripture. "Can't believe you never heard of Kenny Bing."

"And I can't believe you never heard of deodorant." His mouth falls open, but I don't give him a chance to retort. "How did you know he was here? Did one of the EMTs call you?"

Before he can run another line of bullshit, I sense a presence at our side. Jukebox girl, one hand on her hip, stares at Quince. His own eyes are glued to his empty glass.

"I didn't expect to see you again." Her voice is toneless, hard to hear in the noisy BRR.

He doesn't look up. "Welcome to your first Barlow County winter," he mumbles, reaching the limits of his repertoire. With that, he slides roughly out of the booth and lumbers toward the bar. The girl watches his back for a few seconds, then drops into the space he vacated.

"So," she says, pinning me with her thunderous, unblinking eyes, "this joint *The Walking Dead* or what?"

"Could be worse. They could be fast zombies."

"Yeah, well don't let your ass get near their hands." She sets her bottle down and offers her own petite hand. "I'm Thora." From across the table, I can smell tequila on her breath. She's been chasing shots with that Corona.

The warmth of her hand lingers on my own. "Melisende."

"Do you live around here?"

"In Crestview? No."

"Oh." She spreads her hands out on the table. Her manicure flashes in the harsh light, metal-flake gold. "Do you live in town? Like a real town?"

Where I live is even more remote than Crestview, but the county seat is what she's after. "Samuelton is twenty miles east. It's as much of a town as we have in Barlow County. There's a Walmart."

"What about a bus station?"

I have to think for a second. "Greyhound stops at Ray's Thriftway."

"Where's it go?"

"No idea."

"Doesn't matter, I guess." She's quiet for a long time. "Think I could get a ride there?"

For the first time, there's a hitch in her voice. Any time one woman asks another for a ride out of a high-country toilet like BRR, the answer should always be yes. But tonight it's not that simple.

"How do you feel about riding with a dead body?"

Her eyes somehow get even larger.

"I'm a mortuary transport driver. I'm waiting for the medical examiner to release the remains of a man who passed away at the motel."

She gives her pink lip a little tug. "I think I need another shot."

As she gets up, I say, "How do you know Quince?"

She hesitates for a split-second, then straightens. Eyes unfocused. "Who?"

I twist around to gesture toward the bar. Quince has shouldered into his parka again and is deep into a forehead-to-forehead confab with Gert from the Downhill. I didn't see him come in.

"Oh, that guy," Thora says. "He was here earlier."

"What did you mean when you said you didn't expect to see him again?"

She takes so long to answer I wonder if she heard me.

"I thought I'd be gone."

"To the bus stop?"

"Somewhere." Her fingers tap out a quick *rat-a-tat* on the table. "Does this song suck or what?" With that, she makes a beeline for the jukebox. But rather than feed the machine, her arms stretch over her head and her hips start to sway side-to-side. All around BRR, the conversation quiets as geezers turn their attention to the lissome performance.

Only Quince and Gert don't seem to notice. Whatever they're discussing has reached a decision point. They push off the bar. The second they're through the door, I grab my coat.

Outside, I can make out the glow of the emergency lights at Crestview Assisted Living across the highway. Quince and Gert could be ten feet away and I wouldn't spot them.

Doesn't matter. I know where they're going.

With pebbled snow blowing into my face, I follow their stomped path by touch. The light from the nursing home and BRR's neon sign at my back keep me oriented. The going is slow, and by the time I reach the wind shadow cast by the Mercantile my lungs are burning. For a minute or two, I catch my breath under a dying solar-powered light over the store entrance—just bright enough to show Quince and Gert's footprints. When I push on, the wind makes every step feel like a dozen. I find the motel with my face about the time I start worrying I've wandered off line.

At least my nerves have all died of hypothermia.

After a moment to gulp frozen air and regret my life choices, I move along the wall. Around the corner outside Kenny Bing's room, I see the beam of a flashlight is slashing through the darkness from the direction of the lobby.

I press myself against the door. The red points of two cigarettes appear above the flashlight beam, then the vague outlines of two doofuses. They seem to be bickering, though I can't quite make out the words—just vexed tones over the gusting wind. Gert, distinguished by his white hair, jangles a ring of keys just out of Quince's scrabbling grasp. Neither is aware I'm there until I speak.

"What's up, fellas?"

"Cheezus!" Gert spits out his smoke and manages one step before his feet skid out and he pitches face-first into the fender of a parked car. The keys go flying, vanishing without a sound. After a flail, Quince manages to keep his feet. He aims the flashlight at my face. I blink in the blinding glare of what turns out to be his cellphone.

"Girl, what in puckered hell are you doing here?"

"Not breaking and entering, unlike some people."

"We have keys." He shines the light out at the parking lot, for all the good it does. "Had."

I kneel beside Gert, groaning in a knee-high snow drift.

"Ooo bwoke m'nothe," he says through a mouthful of blood.

"You broke your own damn nose." I wave Quince over. "Help me with this jackhole."

With Quince and me at either elbow, Gert manages to hobble back to BRR, complaining the whole way. I can't make out of a word of it. We dump him in my empty booth, then I head to the bar. The BRR-tender offers me a damp towel without comment. Broken noses must be regular occurrence around here.

"That young woman." I say, tilting my head toward the willowy dancer, who's convinced a fogey to join her. He'll need a time machine to find moves necessary for the Aretha song playing on the jukebox.

"Thora Peppermill?"

"You know her?"

"That's the name on her driver's license."

I'm tempted to ask her birthday, probably from the same era as my grandmother's record collection. "How long has she been here?"

"Since I came on at four."

"Alone?"

He glances toward the dance floor. Thora's first partner has given up, but she's gesturing to another white-hair with the posture of a candy cane. "Not if she can help it."

"Did she come in with anyone?"

"You mean that guy Quince has been on about."

"Kenny Bing?"

"That's him. Had that cable travel show back in the nineties."

Don't let Quince hear you say that. "She came in with him?"

"All I know is they were matching Cuervo Gold shooters. After a while, they took off."

"Together?"

He nods. "But she came back alone."

"What time was that?"

"Maybe eight-thirty."

The death call came in at the Old Mortuary a little after nine. Working backward, estimating response time for Fire and Rescue in this weather and time at the scene for an obvious deader, the 911 call couldn't have come in any later than eight.

I nod a thanks, then take the towel back to Gert. Quince tries to slink away, but I shove him onto the bench beside his accomplice and sit down across from them.

"We weren't gonna touch anything," Quince mumbles. Wide-eyed above his reddening towel, Gert bobs his head in agreement.

I should check my wallet. "You drink here a lot, Quince?"

"What's that got to do with anything?"

It occurs to me these fossils calcifying all around us may be Quince's only friends. In BRR's damp heat, my cheeks start to burn.

92

"You saw Kenny here earlier, then stuck around after he left. That's how you came to be waiting for me."

"So?"

"Did you see Fire and Rescue and realize they'd come for your old friend?"

"We weren't exactly friends."

"But you wanted to be."

He peers longingly at his empty glass, still on the table.

"Tell me what happened and I'll buy you a drink." Gert perks up. "Both of you."

Quince takes his time deciding what to do. I'm not sure if it's the promise of booze or a need to unburden himself, but finally he lets out a long, smoky sigh.

"He said he was road-tripping, one last drive to all the places where he performed. I had no idea he ever played this dump. The man is a goddamn legend."

Gert nods. "He's in those life insurance commercials."

Quince's already thin lips vanish against his brown teeth. "Shut yer hole, Gert." He looks at me, and I swear there are fucking tears in his eyes. "He was trying to dance with that girl, making a fool of himself. We all knew she was working him, but he didn't seem to care. Maybe he wanted to be worked, I don't know. But when she suggested they get outta here, his goddamn face about fell into his lap. Get to be our age, there's only one reason an offer like that knocks the wind out of you. I figured Gert could help him out."

"What did you give him?" I ask the old stoner, already guessing the answer.

He pulls the bloody towel away from his face. His nose looks like a used tampon. "V, man. Jus' some V."

The little blue pill. "How many?"

He swallows thickly. "Fife."

"Jesus."

"All he ha' wath a hunert. I din't ha' change."

Viagra at twenty a pop? I'm in the wrong business.

"I suppose your big plan out there was to sneak into his room and remove the evidence."

Gert won't meet my gaze. Neither will Quince.

"You'd have been wasting your time."

"How would you know?"

"Think about it, Mr. Deep Well of Experience."

According to my mortuary textbook, erectile dysfunction meds have joined death by hanging and spinal cord injury as a leading cause of post-mortem priapism. Seek medical attention for erections lasting longer than four hours. Unless you're already dead.

"He probably took them all, dipshit."

That note leaves us in brooding silence. Even the geezer gab has waned. The same jazz guitar song that was playing when I first came in fades away, leaving BRR in a leaden hush. I guess Thora ran out of quarters.

"You gonna tell Dr. Varney?" Quince says at last.

"I shouldn't have to."

"This ain't my job no more, remember?"

His tone is petulant, but none of this should be on me. If he'd stuck to nostalgic reminiscence with his doddering pals, or if Fire and Rescue had simply left someone with the body, I could do my job in peace. Instead I'm stuck cleaning up after a septuagenarian toddler.

I still have a question, one these two can't answer.

But when I look toward the jukebox, Thora Peppermill is gone. I check every table, every booth. The women's room is empty. One of the fogeys acts like I've violated the Geneva Convention when I stick my head through the men's room door. He's alone.

The BRR-tender just shrugs. "Must've left."

Mortuary textbooks don't cover this shit.

* * *

The snow has all but stopped. Only a few fat flakes spiral into a bright glare approaching up the highway. As the light grows, the grinding shriek of a snowplow seems to rip open the night. I spot her then, weighed down by a backpack, struggling through a waist-high drift angling across the parking lot.

"Thora! Stop!"

She can't hear me, or doesn't want to.

"It's not your fault!"

Nearing the road, she waves her arms—as if she has any hope of flagging down the fifty-ton monster roaring up the highway. Too late she realizes her mistake. The instant she turns back, the plow sweeps past and throws a sheet of snow and ice over her. In the space of a heartbeat, she's gone.

I scream for help, then hurtle forward. Almost at once lose I my footing and nearly pull a Gert, catching myself at the last second on the tailgate of a buried pickup. As I hang there, heart pounding, I realize the clouds have broken. A thin streak of moonlight shines down on one of Thora's arms sticking out of the bank of plowed snow.

The fear I'll end up with two bodies to transport chases me, slipping and lurching, across the lot. But I skid to a stop and grasp her arm, she grabs back.

"Hang on, hang on."

Frantic, I plunge my hands into the snow, tossing aside handfuls and frozen chunks. Her desperate mewling rises through the packed slush as I find her shoulder, the back of her head. I push a heavy slab of ice off her backpack, then take hold of the straps and heave.

Not so long ago, the effort would have hopeless. But six months moving the dead has given me an unexpected strength. The compacted snow lets go with a slurp, and I fall backward, dragging Thora after me.

For a long time she just lies there.

"What on earth were you thinking?"

"Fuck if I know." Her voice is ragged. "I just wanted a ride."

* * *

Five or six fogeys, one in a goddamn bathrobe, hobble outside to watch us limp back to BRR. No one offers to help, though one grudgingly holds the door.

"Way to go the extra mile there, grandpa."

At that moment lights blink to life up and down the sad quarter mile of Crestview.

The power is back.

I put Thora in an empty booth as far from Quince and Gert as possible. The BRR-tender brings us fresh coffee and an old blanket from the back. Around the bar, geezers watch her squeeze water from her hair.

"Been hitching since Spokane," she says, without prompting.

"Where to?"

"This girl I know in L.A. said she could get me a job." She glares up at the two mule deer heads. "The last guy I rode with dumped me in this shithole town, so I came in here looking for a ride."

"And Kenny offered you one?"

"Said he was going that way to visit friends in Forest Lawn." She clutches her coffee cup, eyes lost in the steam. "No expectations either. He's the first dude I've met who didn't assume giving me a ride came with privileges. You know?"

"So why'd you go back to his room?"

"He seemed sad. That Quince guy kept talking about how he used to be someone."

The way she says *used to be* opens a void in me, and for a moment I have an idea what Quince might be feeling. *Session musician, game and travel show celebrity. Life insurance hawker.* A man on one last road trip.

"The famous Kenny Bing."

"I'd never heard of him. He was just a nice old man who offered me a ride."

I don't suppose Thora realizes Forest Lawn is a cemetery.

"You called nine-one-one, didn't you?"

"I didn't do anything wrong."

"I don't think you did."

She starts scraping the polish off the middle finger of her right hand. "He had trouble at first, so I tried a few things—" a little color rises in her cheeks "—even turned on a pay-per-view. He ended up going to the bathroom for like twenty minutes. When he came out he was ready to go. Happy, even." Her eyes drop. "Maybe too happy."

That first glimpse through the motel room door flashes through my mind.

"I think part of me knew something was wrong. He was all red and sweaty. I asked if he felt okay, but he kept saying he was fine." When she closes her eyes, the lights in the bar seem to dim. "The last thing he said was, 'Thank you for making tonight a wonderful thing.'"

I'm not surprised to hear she called the front desk and Gert blew her off.

"I tried CPR, but I probably didn't do it right. Maybe it didn't matter. He wasn't breathing, didn't have a heartbeat. He just seemed..." The last of the polish comes off her nail. "...empty. In the end, I used his phone to call nine-one-one, grabbed my stuff, and got out of there. I walked around in the fucking snow until the paramedics showed up, then came back here." She lets out a long breath. "I still need that ride, you know?"

My phone rings—Dr. Varney at long last. He got stuck helping out at a three-car pile-up in Munro, but he's on his way with a deputy. Good thing the plow has been through.

"The scene is secure," I tell him, then disconnect.

Thora is staring at me, worry darkening her thundery eyes. "Who was that?"

"Medical examiner."

"Are you going to tell him about me?"

Same question Quince asked, and in the end I guess I have

the same answer—if for a different reason. I've done what I'm supposed to do. Responded to the death call, and kept Quince from fucking up the scene. Hopefully ensured I get to keep my job for another day. When Dr. Varney releases the body, I'll deliver it to the hospital morgue or the mortuary as required. Beyond that, no one official has reason to think I know the first thing about what happened to Kenny Bing.

"I'm just mortuary transport. He won't even ask." I doubt she has to worry about Quince or Gert either, or the Crestview Assisted Living Geezer Brigade. Not that it will matter once she's gone. "Your name isn't really Thora Peppermill, is it?"

Those big eyes go wide, but then she gives me a shy little smile. "That's just what it says on my ID." With a glance toward the BRR-tender, she adds, "I'll be twenty in January."

"And this job you're going to—"

She chews on her lower lip. "After all this shit, I thought I'd just go back to Spokane."

"Well, Nineteen, I'll be a while—" wrapping up poor Kenny, I don't need to say "—but when I'm done, you still want that ride?"

NO STATIC AT ALL
Jim Winter

"You're her." The man was tall and dark-haired, with a tan jacket hanging loosely from his shoulders. And was that a Steely Dan T-shirt peeking out from under the jacket? "I recognized the voice."

Stephanie took her tea and thanked Emily, the heavily-tattooed owner of the Funky Perk before responding. "I'm who?"

"Her! Steph!"

Here we go again. The weekly ritual of "I know you!"

She looked down at her laptop, waiting for two of her development suites to open. "Me? The girl trying to get some work done before going home?"

"You're Steph the Nightbird on WPRT. I know it!"

She looked down at her watch. It had been a half hour since she left Alex Wilde's studio/Cape Cod home. She wanted to chill and bang out some code for her "real" job before going home and getting some sleep. "Yeah, I'm her. You listen?"

"Every night." The man shoved a hand at her. "I'm Ted, by the way. Big fan."

WPRT had only a smattering of listeners. If Alex had not invested his money well during his years as Monticello's foremost rock jock, he'd have never been able to run WPRT out of his house. At a considerable loss, no less.

Stephanie shifted in her cushy chair to face Ted better. "Well, I am indeed Steph the Nightbird. And yeah, I do the gig overnight for the helluvit." That and Alex sometimes liked to stay up and smoke weed with her.

"That's awesome," Ted gushed. "I can't believe you once played side three of Yes's *Tales from Topographic Oceans.* Do they even allow that anymore?"

"The playlists are based on our whims." She sipped her tea and wished she'd grabbed more honey before sitting down. "And Alex's sometimes. He's the owner. Sit down. Talk to me. What do you want to hear on the show tonight?"

Ted smiled. "Willie Nelson."

That was an odd request. Then again, one night, she made her show a John Coltrane marathon, and no one objected. Not that WPRT had that many listeners during morning and afternoon drive, let alone overnight. But she got a lot of calls that night thanking her for the change-up. The next night, she played all Tom Petty, even the new stuff with Mudcrutch.

"I think I can manage that. I'll mix it in with the death metal I was planning to play. That and half an hour of Mozart."

"How do you guys get away with that?"

Stephanie shrugged. "Remember Mad Alex Wilde on WONK back in the day?" Never mind that, back in that particular day, she had been a teenager. "He had a really good accountant and a really good manager. Runs the station at a loss, does whatever he wants. One night, I called in sick, so he played the Beatles 'Hello Goodbye' on a loop for four hours."

"What about your sponsors?"

"Two funeral homes and a dying Chevy dealership? They're just happy we run the spots in the hours they paid for."

They sat in silence for a while. Stephanie dove into her coding, hoping to have that plugin sent to her corporate masters out in Palo Alto by ten that morning. As of right now, none of them were awake.

"Listen," said Ted, surprising her that he was still there. "This may be a bit forward, but are you doing anything tonight? Before your show?"

She thought for a moment before answering. A listener hadn't hit on her in a while. But this one was cute. And liked Willie Nelson. And anyway, it wasn't like Alex would be jealous. He'd worry more if she was late for her shift. "I could meet you somewhere."

"Chapos in Huron Junction?"

"I can be there at seven-thirty. I have to be at Alex's at midnight." Actually, she had to be at Alex's at one-thirty, but Alex liked to get high with her before the show. How could a girl say no? "Sound good?"

"Seven-thirty then."

"It's a remote job with no set hours," she said after explaining what she did, hopefully in English, for her company. "I get assignments on Mondays and work on them during the week. I've always been a night owl, so I took the gig with Alex when I met him." She stared across the table. When Ted's eyes hadn't glassed over, she counted it as a victory. Most guys, even the ones who developed software like her, grew bored when she talked about her job. Except Alex, but she and Alex bonded over music.

And weed, but mostly music. Some nights, though, it all seemed like static.

"Enough about me," she said. "Tell me about you."

"I sell financing for funerals." He gave her a half-smile. "Not the most glamorous job, but profitable."

"And you obviously like music if you're listening to us."

"Oh, I only listen to you. Some nights, I can't sleep. Your voice helps with that."

"Aw, that's sweet." Over the years, she had learned insomniacs made up the bulk of her audience, insomniacs with eclectic taste in music. "So what do you do with yourself when you're not selling the last piece of real estate we'll ever own?"

He laughed. "I'll have to remember that when I pitch. That's pretty funny." He visibly relaxed. "Sometimes, I fish. Not very well. Obviously, I collect records. Vinyl, actually."

"A lot of what we play is vinyl," she said. "Alex's personal collection. There's this huge room off the studio with just about every recording known to man, half on vinyl. He even has some 78s from before either of us was born. Probably before Alex was born, too."

"How old is he, anyway?"

"He turns seventy this year. He's been on the air since 1965. Used to do that weird disc-jockey voice back when AM was a thing."

"Disc-jockey voice?"

"Twenty minutes after the hour!" She modulated her voice to try and sound like Alex's early persona. "We'll be back in a flash with our classic stacks of wax after this word from Callahan Chevrolet!" She realized, with the voice of a thirty-eight-year-old woman, she sounded nothing like an AM disc jockey from 1969. More like Kermit the Frog having a stroke. "Something like that."

"Wow. How did you get into this?"

"I worked at his favorite record store in my twenties." She frowned at the memory. "There were still a few around back then, despite Napster."

Ted leaned forward and took her hands into his. "What do you say to a nightcap before you go back on the air."

She felt warm, and Ted was probably the most interesting guy she'd met in months. "Would you be disappointed if I said I was a third-date kinda girl?"

"Does this morning count as our first date?"

She shook her head. "No, that was us meeting for the first time." She smiled. "But if you show up at the Funky Perk tomorrow, I'll consider it our second date. I'll even see if Emily will comp you your breakfast. Deal?"

"I suppose so."

"Then be at the Perk at six-thirty."

She showed up at midnight. Alex was waiting for her. Age made him look more rugged than anything. He still had those shaggy bangs she remembered when she first met him at Spin More Records near the Monticello State campus. They had simply gone steel gray from their original brown.

"You're early," he said. "Thought you had a date."

"I did," she said. "First date, so...you know...peck on the lips and a quick goodnight."

Alex laughed. "You just wanted to get here for the pre-show festivities." He led her into the main part of the house, "Alex's Domain," she and the other jocks called it. On the speakers, they could hear Charlie White, the late-night jock, doing his jazz show.

"Taped again?" she asked, accepting a joint from Alex.

Alex lit her joint, then his own, and held in some of the smoke for a moment. "Smooth." He took a few short breaths, the way he always did when he had some particularly strong stuff. "I haven't seen Charlie in four months, but he sends me his recorded shows for the week every Friday at four like clockwork."

"Slacker," said Stephanie after taking another hit.

"In fact," said Alex, "you're the only jock that still comes in regularly. And I know it's not because you enjoy talking to the overnight lurkers. Hell, even *I* tape my shows ahead of time. Takes me about two hours once I have the playlists and commercial spots queued."

She took a long pull on the joint and let the smoke work its magic in her lungs. Exhaling, she said, "I like being unpredictable on the air. I was thinking of playing some death metal tonight. My date wants me to play Willie Nelson."

"Go ahead and play Willie," said Alex, "but I have a request."

"Yes?"

"Shove Kaminski Chevrolet from two-seventeen to two-forty-five and play Pink Floyd's *Wish You Were Here* all the way through."

"Let me guess. This is another bucket list thing you want to do, and you think I'm just going to go along with it."

"You're not?"

"I didn't say that."

They had finished making love as "Have a Cigar" kicked in. Alex's lovemaking never set the night on fire, but it was always interesting. What age had taken from him he made up for by paying more attention to her. And to celebrate their latest round, they did indeed each have a cigar.

"You're a dork," she said after blowing a stream of smoke toward the ceiling. "Smoking a cigar during 'Have a Cigar'?"

Alex laughed. "I didn't hear you complaining."

"I wasn't. I just think you're a dork for ending with a pair of cigars during that song."

After a few quick puffs, he lay his cigar aside. "I have a proposition."

"You want me to put on side two of *Meddle* and go at it again? You have a Floyd fetish tonight?"

"No." He sat up, grunting as his back protested. "Listen, the winters in this town are getting to me. I'm thinking of moving to Florida."

Now it was Stephanie who sat up. "Am I out of a job?"

Alex laughed again. "You've got that computer crap you can do from anywhere in the country. The world, if I'm not mistaken. What it is it, anyway? Some blogging platform?"

"Something like that."

"Good. Come with me. You can write code on the beach.

Make a dirty old man happy in his remaining days."

She sat in silence, wrapping her arms around her knees.

"Steph, if you don't want to come, just say so. I'll even let you run the station if you want to stay. I just thought..."

"I have one date, and suddenly you're threatened." The way he arched his eyebrows confirmed her suspicions. "I knew it. You know you were thirty-two when I was born. You were in your mid-fifties the first time we slept together. And did your wife ever find out?"

"Oh, she left me long before she knew you even existed. It was all the other women she left me over." He rolled onto his side. "And I've never asked you about other men. I even stayed away when you were married. But would you believe you've been the only one for the last seven years?"

"If you tell me I'm like a daughter to you, I'm putting on my clothes and leaving. You can just put 'Hello, Goodbye' on a loop while you look for a new overnight jock."

"I won't go that far," he said. "But you're my only real friend."

"Don't get maudlin on me, Madman. What do you want? Are you proposing to me?"

"Nothing like that. Do you know everything I own?"

Did she? She knew he owned a lot of property, rented out apartments in other cities, had a few restaurants. In fact, Alex Wilde, the investor, had done quite well for himself. "I know some of it."

"I want you to have it. And all you have to do is come with me to Siesta Key."

"What's this about? You have a daughter."

"I talk to my ex more than to her. Which is to say I still talk to Joy occasionally. Shared suffering, even if we were each other's reason to suffer. And the ex complains she never talks to her, either. Susan is lost to both of us. I've even tried private detectives."

She shifted and pushed him back down onto the bed so she

could hover over him. "You plan to give your fortune to me if I become an exclusive friends with benefits. Is that it?"

He reached up and patted her on the cheek. "It's more than that, girlie. You could have walked out of here anytime you wanted, and yet you stick around. And don't tell me you like having a sweaty, wheezy old man pawing you for his own pleasure. You like the music. It's always been the music with us."

"Sometimes, it's just static." She puffed a little more on her cigar. "Some nights, it's all static. I never know what you really want from me. Think about it. You gave me away at my wedding."

"And I got you drunk the day your separation agreement came in the mail. You didn't even wait for the divorce papers to resume our little arrangement."

He had her there.

"I want out of this damn house," he said. "And I can't handle another January of wind off Lake Erie or ice on the Inland Parkway. My bones already hurt, and it's November."

She looked into his eyes and saw something else there. Fear. "What else is it, Alex? You're talking to me, but I'm only hearing more static."

He looked away. "I'm dying. Slowly."

" *What?* "

"There's a spot on my lungs. Damn doctors want to cut a piece out of it, but I remember they carved up my dad like that. Two packs a day and a job at Johnson Steel when the old mill still existed. All that tobacco and coal smoke...He died screaming. I'd at least like to die someplace warm with a beautiful woman at my side."

She punched him in the chest. "You bastard. You're leaving me."

He laughed, then coughed. "A piece at a time." He sat up and pushed her back so she had to lean back on her hands. "Do you like our little arrangement?"

"Yes, but you know I never want to get married again."

"You don't have to. Unless you want to make sure everything goes to you. The only thing that has to change, Stephanie, is the location. We can still run the station from Siesta Key. Tape our shows. Maybe even go to podcast. You can handle that, right?"

"Maybe."

"Promise me you'll think about it."

She leaned forward and pushed him back again, pinning him to the bed. "How long?"

"Two years if I don't do anything. And I've seen what chemo does to a man."

She leaned down and kissed him hard. "Then let's take every moment you have left and have us a little party."

He ran his hand down her back. "What say we consummate the deal with another go?"

The album had gone into the final sections of "Shine on You Crazy Diamond."

"What about Kaminski Chevrolet's spot?"

"Fuck 'em," said Alex, working the sheet out from under Stephanie. "They're late on their bill."

Someone grabbed her arm as soon as she opened her car door. With an instinct only techies had, she kicked the door shut again to protect her laptop, stashed out of sight beneath the driver's seat. A hand spun her around to face someone in a ski mask.

Fear went through her like an electric shock even as one stubbornly rational part of her mind said, *A ski mask? Really? Who wears a ski mask anymore?*

The fear answered in short order. *A mugger. A car thief. A rapist.* She didn't wait for the man to make a move. Her knee came up into his balls. Before he could double over, she jabbed her car keys into his eye. The man screamed.

"You bitch! You fucking bitch!"

Bitch she may be, but he was already doubled over and half blind. Had she left her car door open, a tire iron would lay within reach. Instead, she punched the attacker in the side of the head. Freed, she ran toward the Funky Perk.

Emily had heard the screaming and come running out waving a frying pan. "Hey, you!"

The attacker had not even pivoted to chase Stephanie when the pan—solid cast-iron—slammed into the side of his face. He went down, sprawling on the broken asphalt of the Perk's parking lot.

Emily knelt at the man's side. "Sonofabitch. Attack someone in my parking lot."

She peeled the ski mask off as Stephanie called 911. She stopped when she saw the guy's face, and even bloody and beginning to swell on one side, she recognized him. Her stomach turned, and she nearly dropped the phone. "Ted?"

"Seriously," said Ted from inside the interrogation room, "someone paid me to do it. You need to talk to her."

Stephanie watched as her date, the one she pecked on the cheek the night before and told to meet her at the Funky Perk that morning, sat under the glower of two Midtown cops, one a tall black male, the other a small, compact female who looked like she could rip Ted's head off without breaking a sweat. They weren't playing good cop/bad cop, either.

"Someone paid you to beat up a woman you just met the night before," said Harris, the female cop. "She says you had a date last night before her shift, and that you were supposed to meet for breakfast this morning."

"We had a date last night," said Ted.

"Well, he got that right," said Stephanie to Grayson, a female plainclothes officer who stood with her behind the one-way glass watching with her arms folded. "We were supposed to meet *inside* the Perk."

Grayson gave her a tight smile, her dark face betraying little amusement.

"What about the breakfast date?" asked Lincoln, the male cop.

"That was a ruse," said Ted. "This woman paid me to scare her away."

"From what? She live in your building? Stealing your laundry? Your morning paper?"

"Does anyone read newspapers anymore?" asked Lincoln.

Ted gave a sheepish smile. "This woman said she's screwing her boss for money."

Stephanie paled. "I am not!"

Grayson turned to her, her eyes now narrow. "Is that true? Are you sleeping with your employer?"

Stephanie frowned. "We've been...We've had an informal relationship for about twenty years. It was never about the money. We love music, any music."

"When did you meet?" Grayson's tone was sharp, her words rapid.

"Back when I was in college," said Stephanie. "At the old Spin More Records down by Monticello State."

"That head shop?"

Stephanie felt her cheeks warm. "They closed in 2005, so yes, I can admit it was a head shop."

"Doesn't matter if you admit it or not." Grayson winked. "Not a record person, but I bought some...merchandise there in college." She straightened. "So...What? Older man wants to take you in the back room with a bag of weed and some old Isley Brothers vinyl and show you how he might have hooked up with Paula Abdul back in the day?"

Actually, it had been Cream, and Alex said he had hooked up with Grace Slick. "Something like that. We're friends. With benefits. I work for him because I get bored writing code all day. I've always preferred the night. Probably why I never had kids."

Grayson's posture tightened. "Who's this woman who wants to run you off?"

Stephanie shrugged. "Ex-wife maybe? He has a daughter neither he *nor* his ex ever hear from. Susan, I think. Obsessed fan? Maybe someone he played 'Misty' for? I'm not stupid. I know Alex has always had appetites that one woman can't satisfy. Or used to, anyway."

"Maybe he still does."

She stiffened when Alex met her at the door with a hug.

"What's wrong?" he said. "I heard what happened at the Perk. Are you okay?"

When he let go, she stepped back, folding her arms. "You said I've been the only one you've been with since your divorce. Was that bullshit?"

Alex's face sagged. "Steph, I wouldn't lie to you, but it's not like you haven't had other men. What's wrong?"

"Someone hired Ted to scare me away from you. Said her name was Mandy."

"I don't know a Mandy," he said. "Come inside. Sit down."

She put her hand up. "No. All I know is Ted told the police some woman named Mandy hired him to scare me off because she knew you and I have been sleeping together."

"Are you going to believe a stalker you just met or a man you've known for twenty years?"

"*Do* I know you? You were married when we met. And somehow, I still let you talk me into that first time in that back room."

"Is it that you don't trust me?" He looked up at the ceiling for a moment. "Have I ever hidden anything from you? You knew I was married our first time together. I never made a move on you when you were married or even for a year after your divorce. I never asked you for anything more than your company and anything you felt like giving."

"Well, no one's ever attacked me in a parking lot and blamed you for it." She shoved her hands in her pocket. "Was Florida bullshit?"

"Stephanie, I've always known you were never about the money. That's why I asked. Every other woman I've met was looking for a payday. You're the only one I trust."

She felt the tears welling up in her eyes. "That makes one of us." She turned and walked back toward the Perk, four blocks up the street. In her car, she sat with her head on the steering wheel, sobbing. Eventually, she drove back to her place.

She'd be spending a lot of time there.

Her crappy little apartment had become crappier. She found the door open, the lock busted, and her furniture overturned. The TV sported a huge spider-web crack in the center, and all her CDs and vinyl had been thrown around the room.

Food lay on the floor in front of the open refrigerator in what passed for her kitchen. Stephanie did not even feel the urge to cry. She dialed 911, told the dispatcher everything she needed to know about the place, then proceeded to pick up the albums on the couch. One had to sit somewhere, and the intruder had left few options.

She called her landlord and explained about the lock while waiting for the police. Then she called Alex. "Mandy had our friend destroy my apartment," she told his voicemail. "I hope you're happy." She clicked off.

Two officers arrived five minutes later. They went through the place while waiting for a city detective to show up. Detective Grayson appeared ten minutes after them, a scowl on her face.

"Boy," said the plainclothes officer, "either that Ted hates you or whoever hired him does."

Stephanie's phone buzzed. She did not answer it, not even

when she saw Alex's number. "I'm guessing he did this over-night. Before he attacked me at the Perk."

"Does this building have video security?" asked Grayson.

"I think so. The foyer and the parking lot." Her phone buzzed again. "My landlord won't put in coded locks, but he'll spend hours tinkering with those damn cameras. He has it fed to his house."

"Let's call him."

It took maybe an hour for Howard, Stephanie's landlord, to show up with his laptop. He had created his own surveillance system that kept recordings going back two weeks from any given moment. Grayson interrupted his complaining about the mess and ordered him to boot up his laptop and bring up the surveillance footage.

"She was with the suspect between seven-thirty and ten," said Grayson, who stood behind the couch shoulder-surfing Howard. "So let's start from seven last night."

Howard queued up the recording to playback from 7:03 p.m. the previous night, and fast-forwarded. "We'll stop it each time someone comes in or out of the building or the parking lot."

On one side of Howard's laptop screen, an image of the building's parking lot flickered. On the other, the front foyer sat in something of a glare from the naked bulb in the ceiling.

"Sorry about the lighting," he said. "I just use it to see who's coming and going when there's a complaint."

"Ever have to use it?"

"Yes," Stephanie and Howard said in unison.

"That lush I rented apartment E to," said Howard. "Got three noise complaints, a police report, and had to call the exterminator. Caught her pissing in the bushes and scrawling graffiti on another tenant's door. Earned her a three-day notice to vacate."

They started with Stephanie leaving for the night, dressed in the same blouse and jeans she now wore, though even in the grainy footage, they looked a little fresher.

At about eight or so, someone pulled into the lot in a Chevy Malibu. A black man came through the door a minute later.

"Daryl," said Stephanie. "LaShonda's boyfriend. Either he'll leave about ten or early the next morning. I usually pass him in the parking lot in the morning."

"Does he live here?" asked Howard, an edge in his voice.

"Never mind that," said Grayson. "Any problems with him?"

"Only when LaShonda's drunk," said Stephanie. "Sometimes, she gets jealous when she's had too much tequila."

Howard shrugged and fast-forwarded. They stopped each time someone came through the door. Every time, Stephanie could identify the person as one of her neighbors or a frequent visitor. LaShonda apparently did not have a fight with Daryl that night as, from 11:46 p.m. to almost eight the following morning, no one entered or left the lot or the building, save for a Monticello Police cruiser that pulled in at 2:34 a.m. The officer within had his dome light on and was studying his laptop.

"Paperwork," said Grayson. "Looks like he's working overnight power shift, seven to three."

Stephanie did not envy the officer. People began leaving for work after 8 a.m. A few utility workers from First Energy and Verizon showed up shortly after nine. And then someone wearing a jacket similar to Ted's appeared. He did not come through the parking lot but marched straight through the front door. He had on a Tigers ball cap pulled low and large sunglasses.

"That your boyfriend?" asked Howard.

"No," said Stephanie.

Grayson chuckled. "Poor choice of words. But it can't be him."

"Still, he wore that jacket, or a similar one, to the Perk yesterday morning, but she's right. It can't be him."

"Why?" said Howard.

"Because Ted Morgan has been in police custody since around seven this morning."

Stephanie's phone vibrated again, third time that hour. She looked down. Two missed calls and a text from Alex: *Please call me. Emergency.*

She did not bother calling. As soon as she finished up with Grayson, she jumped in her car and sped off toward Alex's. On most nights she parked at the Perk, partly so it would look like Emily was not alone when she opened the shop. Tonight, she went straight for the house and Alex.

Along the way, she put on WPRT, hoping she'd hear the night jock's prerecorded show. Instead, she heard Steely Dan's "FM," boasting "No static at all." Oh, it had static all right. Someone had put it on a loop. On nights she parked at Alex's, she always found room behind his aging Ram pickup. Tonight, a Hyundai with a sagging bumper and faded paint job sat in the way. She rolled up onto the curb stopping inches from the fire hydrant out front.

Good, she thought, *let it get the cops' attention.* She bounded up the front lawn and through the front door like she had done a thousand times before. "Alex?"

No response came except for "FM" starting over again.

She decided to let Alex and his unknown visitor know she was there, just in case they were too busy. Canceling the loop, she found another Steely Dan song to play, "Don't Take Me Alive."

No sooner had the opening chords begun than a woman charged out of the main part of the house swinging a tire iron. Stephanie grabbed the office chair—there for any jock who still did their show live—and raised it up as a makeshift shield. The chair caught the tire iron as it came down.

Stephanie put all her strength into a push that jammed the chair into the woman's face. She screamed and staggered backwards. Stephanie pushed her back into Alex's Domain, into the living room. When she had some room to swing, she brought the chair down and pinned her chest and arm.

The woman tried to hold onto the tire iron, but Stephanie kicked it away. The woman screamed again. On the couch in the next room, Alex sat up, blood pouring from his nose and forehead. His face had turned as gray as his hair, and his eyes looked cloudy. Angry, she drew back her foot and aimed squarely for the woman's head.

"Stop," Alex croaked.

"Lie down, Alex. This woman tried to kill you. She had Ted attack me."

"I know." He finally pulled himself upright. "She's my daughter. Amanda. Mandy. We never called her that. That's why I never recognized the name earlier."

"You bitch," the woman on the floor said through a broken nose. "You're fucking him for my money."

Alex leaned forward, elbows on knees and trying to breathe normally. "She's also never getting back into the will. I can tell you that."

"You're the one who trashed my apartment." Stephanie pressed a boot against Mandy's windpipe. "Nice disguise. Did you know your father was dying?"

"I know you've been fucking him," she snarled, struggling to get out from under the chair. She began wheezing when Stephanie leaned her full weight into it.

"Stop," said Alex again, this time breathing hard. "You'll kill her."

"She nearly killed you."

He wheezed again then broke into a rasping cough. "I told you. I'm dying anyway."

She threw the chair aside, but she didn't help Amanda up. "You knew?"

"I suspected. Like I said, we never called her Mandy."

"Mother did," said Amanda, now up on her knees. "Oh, God, I think you broke my nose."

"You broke his," said Stephanie.

Alex stood shakily and braced himself against the couch. His blood stained the cushions where he had lain. "And you never call your mother, either. Why this, Amanda? Why get your brother to attack this woman? Why didn't you call?"

"Brother?" Now Stephanie had trouble standing. "Ted's your brother?" She glared at Alex. "You never told me about this."

"*Half*-brother," said Amanda, grunting as she climbed to her feet. "Mom had a son when she and him met," she jutted her chin in Alex's direction, "This was his idea."

Stephanie felt the room begin to spin. "You never told me any of this."

"I told you Amanda had issues," said Alex. "That was why she fell out of touch with me and her mother."

"You never talk to Mother." Amanda spun, almost falling.

"Talk to her every day," said Alex. "It's you who never talks to her."

"Ted said..."

"Ted is a manipulative little bastard." Alex looked at Stephanie, his eyes starting to clear. "His old man had custody, but even he worried. Had a stepdaughter of his own who said she thought he was creepy." He stumbled over to Stephanie and put his hands on her shoulders. "Steph, let me handle her. You go on home, and I'll see you tonight."

Stephanie raised the phone to her ear.

She ignored him.

"You call the police, and our arrangement is off."

She felt a tight, joyless smile pull at her lips. Looking at Amanda's own bleeding face, she said, "That ended the moment your stepson attacked me." She thumbed the call icon and waited for 911 to answer.

Alex looked ready to cry, but for some reason, Stephanie did not feel it.

For the first time in twenty years, she realized she was free. She had never even realized she wasn't until now.

"Nine-one-one, what is your emergency?"

She gave Alex's address. "I'd like to report an intruder. She's violent but subdued now."

And with that, she knew WPRT was off the air. No more overnight shifts. No pre-show joints or sex during twenty-minute progressive rock epics. No free-form playlists wondering if Kaminski Chevrolet paid their advertising bill.

And no static at all.

WEST OF HOLLYWOOD
Libby Cudmore

Everyone in Los Angeles is a goddamn mark. Head over to Hollywood and the jobs just get easier. Pretend to be a casting director and you had an endless parade of beauties lined up outside your bedroom. Pretend to be an investor and you'll have fifteen grand of Daddy's money in your bank account before you can finish the lunch the screenwriters paid for. And that was before crowdfunding. Crowdfunding made everyone into con artists.

Noah and I pulled cons because we could. Because it was fun. Because we were smart. I don't even remember how we got hooked up, but when we did, it was like fire and gasoline. A year of money and sex and adrenaline, and then one day he was gone. His apartment was cleared out, he left no forwarding address. For years I wondered if he'd been killed, if he'd been caught, if he ever really existed. Then they invented Facebook.

It turned out Noah had married a small-town beauty queen and settled into a respectable life. Maybe that was the longest pull of all. Life's a long con, if you want to get wine-drunk freshman-year philosophy major about it. He even directed his daughter's school plays. A step up for a man who couldn't even land a regional car commercial fifteen years go. And me— well, in Hollywood, there's always work at a coffee shop if

119

you're an early riser who doesn't skip a shift to read a line for a shampoo commercial or play yet another battered cop-show hooker.

So imagine my surprise when I looked up and saw Noah in my line. Or maybe it wasn't Noah, just a pre-espresso hallucination. I used to think I saw him all the time, called out to him for the first couple of years. It was never him. I stopped asking after a while. He was gone, just like the money. It never lasts as long as you think it will.

But whoever this was two people back from my register, Noah or just another forty-something Midwestern dreamer, he had given himself over to the grey that crept into his temples at thirty-two, swapped out ice-blue contact lenses for hipster glasses. "Americano," he said when he reached me. "Make it two. And take your break. We've got some catching up to do."

There wasn't even time to catch up. The job was coming up quick; every second had to go into planning. "I'm just in town for the weekend," he said in a low voice when we'd settled into the back booth. "Told my wife I'm at a teacher's convention; there's one at the Staples Center. I got the tote bag and the schedule as cover."

"What's the job?" I asked. I didn't want to hear about his wife. Didn't want to hear about his life. Didn't want to be reminded that he moved on from the good thing we had.

"It's nothing fancy," he said. "If we get twenty grand, I'd be surprised. But it's not about the money."

We'd always subsisted on small jobs, cruise ship scams on rich bachelors, pawned jewelry a producer's wife wouldn't notice missing after a party. It's not a crime to take advantage of someone with too much money and not enough sense. We were strippers and investors, promise boys and wealthy young heiresses. And the money was good, sure, but we were better. In a city where the intoxicant of your choice was just a wink and a whisper away, he was my drug. "It never was," I said.

And there it was, laid bare on the table. He gave me a flat smile with nothing behind it. "Marcus DeVille," he said. "Remember him?"

Sure, I remembered Marcus. He and Noah had been roommates for a time in a closet in Culver City. They were even friends for a short while, two handsome young men trying to make it in the business. Marcus eventually got cast on some one-season cop show, then as a bit player in a couple of movies, then as second lead on another pile of Fox drivel now in its fifth season. But what did he have to do with this?

"Talked to my friend Rob the other day," he continued. "Now Marcus wants to direct, of course. Says he wants to do one of those movies with the 'blow budget,' some big dumb nostalgic action set piece."

"You're trying to get back in the business?" I asked.

"I'm not done yet," he said. "He confessed to Rob that in all those years, he was deleting my callbacks." He sank back against his chair like the weight of this revelation was too much to bear. "A few commercials, a couple episodes of *Law & Order*, a part in *School Ties*. Apparently, Marcus would take my messages and pretend to be me, tell him I wasn't available for those shooting days. Now I know why Dolores dropped me."

Dolores was his agent, a chain-smoking ex-New Yorker. I remember the call. I remember his protests. Now it all made sense. "Motherfucker," I said.

"Yeah," he said. "So this is payback."

The gig seemed easy enough. Noah would pose as a screenwriter, trusting that he was long enough gone that Marcus wouldn't recognize him. I'd use a skimmer when Noah's card failed and Marcus bought the coffee. Anything to show off how much money he had. Old rich men won't throw a penny into the tip jar, but a young one will toss in a fifty and make sure everyone bears witness to his generosity. We'd pull the cash from his account that night and Noah would be back in his hotel room in time to get a full night's sleep before whatever panel on curriculum structure he was supposed to be at. And I'd be back at the coffee shop. Ten grand wasn't going to get me far in this town.

Marcus came in jittery. He forgot his wallet. I ducked into the back and let Lisa take his order. Noah played through the whole scene anyways. I dragged an ear while I did side work. Coke talk. Time—or, more likely, hair dye and a good surgeon—had been surprisingly good to him; only a few extra lines around his eyes betrayed any clock at all.

The project was like every other project men his age wanted to make, full of allegories about his father and Hitler alongside special effects and barely-legal actresses. Noah assured him it would play huge in Hong Kong, where his investors lived. But Noah was rusty, and I think the coke did more to sell the idea than he did. Marcus wanted us to meet his screenwriting partner.

"A party in the hills tomorrow night," Noah said after Marcus had left. "Just like old times."

I hit up a second-hand store that bought wardrobe collections off studio backlots and picked up the cheapest, ugliest cocktail dress I could find in my size. I had a lot to choose from, and settled on an asymmetrical black one-shoulder number with a vomit-spatter of sequins. It cost more than I would ever spend on a dress, but that was the cost of looking the part. And if we couldn't get the money up front, there would always be a watch to snatch.

I met Noah at his hotel room. I had roommates, we couldn't

meet there, and he could expense account some room service. He walked me through the plan. It felt as though no time had passed at all. The only difference was that the hotel rooms were nicer.

And when he kissed me, I let him.

Noah hit the pillow like he'd been blasted out of a cannon. "Wow," was all he could say. "Wow. That. That was incredible."

I nestled my head into the crook of his shoulder. He still smelled the same, aftershave and sandalwood and coffee. The hair on his chest had gone soft and grey; I had to resist the urge to rake my fingers through it like fresh-cut grass. "So why didn't we work out?" I asked before I could stop myself.

He leaned his head into my hair, kissed my forehead. "Remember doing blow at that producer's party in Santa Monica?" he said. "How incredible that felt?"

That was a good night. I had never done coke before, but we were fresh off a week-long con in wine country and I felt invincible. The coke only amplified that feeling. Like I was made of stars. Like I could live forever. Like Noah was my one true love, my soul mate. We never bothered with labels, never even bothered with the formalities of love. What we had was deeper. We had the sort of trust you find in war trenches. Love was a liability. I knew that when he broke my heart.

He continued. "That's what it felt like when I was with you," he said. "Every goddamn minute. But if you do nothing but snort coke, eventually your heart will give out. It's not that I didn't love you—I did—but we couldn't sustain. So yeah, life with Carina is comfortably dull. But that's rehab. I don't wake up every morning wondering if this is the day we'll get caught, we'll get killed."

If he gave me that line twenty years ago, I wouldn't have believed him. Probably would have slapped him. But these days it made sense. Most of the cons we had come up with were dead or in prison. The best had retired. Guess that made us among the Academy's choice. The last left to pull one final job.

Good to know these Hollywood parties hadn't changed in the twenty years since we quit the scene. New phones, sure, and tackier clothes, but the same pin-straight blondes, the same bored bartenders, the same loud douchebags with the same scruffy faces. Maybe this was some straight-up *Groundhog Day* bullshit and I was stuck in a time loop. Or maybe time doesn't really move so quickly after all.

Noah vanished to talk shop and almost immediately I was surrounded by men with shark smiles and dead eyes. I wasn't in the mood, but I had to pretend to be in the mood if I was going to get out of here alive.

I made my way to the food. A man in a pink shirt printed with tiny bicycles followed. "What brings you here?" he asked.

I handed him one of my cards—with the name Monica—and slathered on a southern accent. "My daughter, Claire, is a *brilliant* actress," I said. "She's so beautiful too, and a cheerleader. She did some regional ads, you know, like car lots, and we thought, well hell, we might as well come out here and try."

"Where is she?" he said.

I gestured vaguely into the living room. "I told her to go make some friends," I said. "I thought maybe if she talked to some of the models here they might be able to help her find some work. We're so new here, I don't know anyone but I thought, why not try to meet some people."

"Absolutely," he said. He stood up and handed me a card. I could already see he was hunting for the imaginary Claire, eyes hungry, all but licking his lips at the prospects, dick hard in his linen slacks. "I'll look for her, but just in case, why don't you plan to bring her by on Thursday?"

"I will do that," I said. "So nice to meet a gentleman out here."

He didn't reply. He was already looking for Claire.

I filled a plate up with sushi and went out to the pool. "Didn't I just see you on a billboard over the strip?" asked a man in an orange suit.

Another card, a new accent. Swedish. I sent him to get me more sushi and he went quickly. On my way back inside I handed out two more cards, Gina, the nightclub owner and Danielle, another actress, new in town. I took every card handed to me. I'd think of something to do with them later.

Noah texted me. *Money in hand*, he said. *Cash.*

The best thing about these hipster fucks is they all want to do everything old school, typewriters and cheap cigarettes and bags of cash. I was just surprised he didn't make arrangements to slip it under the door of the men's room.

I want a souvenir, I texted.

Let's find a bedroom, he replied.

First couple bedroom doors were locked. Occupied, I could hear the mechanical sounds of a faked orgasm. I heard moaning from the bathroom and found the door unlocked, a smack-skinny model crumpled next to the toilet. "Hold my hair," she said.

I obeyed. "Lemme get that necklace out of the way." I said. "Don't want to puke on that."

I unclasped the necklace. Just a little gold thing, a couple diamonds, could even be fake. But it was pretty, and she wouldn't miss it. I tucked it in my bag with one hand while I held back her hair with the other. She retched into the bowl. There wasn't much left to puke up.

"Let me call you a cab," I said when she was finished. "Before some creep tries to take you home."

"Nah, it's cool," she said, staggering to her feet. She took off her heels and wobbled to the sink and rinsed her mouth. "Purse?"

I picked up her purse. She didn't say anything about the necklace. She fixed her lipstick and found a mint and kissed me on the cheek by way of thanks and then she was gone. I had my souvenir. Now we had to find one for him.

Marcus was passed out on the bed of the back guest room, bare ass up. Not an uncommon scene at these parties, although it's always rude when the host does it so early in the night. Noah rifled through his watch box like old baseball cards, looking for something to make the night profitable. It took me a few minutes to notice that no sounds came out of Marcus. I touched his neck. Cold.

"Noah," I breathed. "He's dead."

We left. We figured the cops would be called in the morning when the housekeeper tried to pull up the blankets, but by the time we got back to the hotel, the news had already hit the lobby. Twitter lit up like a goddamn sparkler. Facebook hit the meme game early. Too young, too soon, too tragic. R.I.P., *just heard the news, heartbroken.* The Russians, the Mole People, the Starwhackers got him. It was all disgusting in a way I couldn't quite pinpoint.

We still had two of his watches. "Dump 'em," I said.

"Lenny still in business?"

"Should be."

Noah made a couple calls to pawn shops we used to frequent. Places that gave vague IDs and fake names to cops, bought and sold on an underground network. The cash would be quick and shoddy, but the money didn't matter now. All that mattered was getting rid of any evidence.

I had the necklace I lifted. I rooted through Noah's jacket pockets to find the watch. I came back with an Altoids tin and popped it open. I could use a couple to settle my stomach.

But there weren't any mints. Instead, there were three small packets of powder. Not very much in each, barely a fingernail. But Noah was never a cokehead; other than the Santa Monica party, we only did it once or twice.

"Carfentanil," Noah said behind me. "Elephant tranquilizers. Or rather, coke laced with it. There was a lockdown drill at school, I found it in a student's backpack. I did the right thing by taking it off him."

"So why do you still have it?" I asked.

I knew the answer before he even opened his mouth. "No," I said. "No, Noah, this isn't you. This isn't us. Please tell me…" I swallowed dry. "Please tell me you didn't kill him."

He looked at me with an expression I couldn't read, like he had ice running through the core of his soul. "I didn't force him to take anything, if that's what you're asking," he said. "I just drew the lines. He chose to cross them. Or, snort them, if you will."

It was never about the money. It had always been about vengeance, about violence. And he'd roped me into it, conned me as easily as he'd conned Marcus. He'd go back to Tracy with blood on his hands that he called justice and I'd be left here with a couple grand in my account and a secret that would eat away at me for the rest of my life. He had used me. Maybe he'd always been using me, a lie about partners, about love.

But now I had to wonder if he was going to kill me to keep his secret. For the first time in my life, I was scared of him. But there wasn't time to be scared. I had to make myself invaluable, had to convince him that I could be trusted with this secret the way I had been trusted with every other secret. I just had to get through the night.

I forced a smile. I played a character. I wrapped my arms around his neck and whispered in his ear. "Then let's celebrate," I cooed. "To the biggest job of all."

* * *

I hated how incredible the sex was. I hated my own desire, hated how quickly my own adrenaline caught fire. Maybe I was no better, racking up sins I couldn't pay down. But it all felt too good. Like champagne. Like cocaine. Like fireworks at midnight on New Year's Eve. I couldn't stop myself.

But I could stop him. He could get away with murder or he could get away with the money. Not both. He had shown he couldn't make those choices. I could make them for him. I was always the smarter of the two of us, and maybe that's what hurt the most about this. That he'd managed to surprise me, managed to outthink a plan. I would never let that happen again. Not with him or with any other man.

I begged for more. I surprised him in the shower, popped another bottle of champagne, kept refilling his glass until around 3 a.m. when he finally turned over and fell asleep hard. Now was my chance. I only had one getaway.

I took all the money. I ditched my phone so he couldn't call me. I took the club owner Gina's ID. I always liked her best. She was better than me; college-educated, rode horses, had sisters she liked and a family who loved her. The lives I pretended to live were always so much better than my own, but I could build a new one.

The money would help.

So would getting the hell out of Hollywood.

DON'T TAKE ME ALIVE
Aaron Erickson

It was finally time to meet Vanessa Courtwright face to face. Reaching out to her account at the newspaper, I used my academic majors in Animal Behavior and Ecology as a source of insight into the "killer's" motivations. I proposed that I could help her understand the purpose of the killings, from an evolutionist's perspective. I had to reveal more of myself than I would have preferred, in order to convince her to meet, but there was no suitable alternative to her as an asset that I could groom to act as my voice to the world.

I had painstakingly pored over the columns of several local news writers, seeking one who might possess the flexibility and intelligence to understand my motivations. Vanessa's work consistently displayed a patience and openness to unfamiliar ideas. She did not insert herself into the story as an egotist might, and she did not seek to judge those with unconventional vision.

Though I believed she might have some faint suspicion as to who I truly was, I was not prepared to expose my true identity as *Homo Superior* until I trusted that she could accept the rationale behind my actions. I had scouted a coffee shop with good visibility, limited opportunities to stage an ambush, and numerous paths of egress. She did not seem foolish enough to squander this exclusive opportunity, but I had no reason to blindly trust her discretion. I waited across the street to see her arrive and walk inside. She appeared to be alone. This meeting would proceed as planned.

She smiled warmly as I sat down. "Thank you for meeting with me," she said. "I am sure someone with your...outlook is not prone to seeking out face-to-face discussions like this. From your correspondence, you seem particularly uncomfortable with the population density here in the city."

I smiled in return. "It is every bit as much the population composition as it is the density," I politely corrected her. "The human population is largely unregulated by natural selection. The result is the passing of disadvantageous genes through generations. The species lacks a predator to remove the weak and unfit. Other measures have failed as well, since agricultural advances have rendered scarcity of food to be more of an economic tool than a population-limiting factor."

She frowned as she considered my point. "Wouldn't disease continue to keep the population in check?"

That was an insightful, if innocent, response. She was showing promise.

I assumed a smile while replying, "The plagues failed. Those lacking either the physical fortitude to endure the disease or the imagination to conjure a cure were destined to succumb to a purge upon the species, but the weak-hearted nature of humanity disrupted genetic progress."

Her face changed to an expression that I was unable to read. She did not ask me to stop, or even explain. In fact, she didn't speak at all, which I interpreted as encouragement to continue.

"The dispassionately calculating blade of evolution was dulled by the softer sensibilities of better men, men who were, in fact, fit for survival. Empathy and compassion overwhelmed survival instinct. Those blessed with vision discovered treatments, developing cures and vaccines. Evolution was prepared to lift these men to the apex of humanity, but they defied natural selection by spreading their gift too widely and sharing the means of survival. They saved the unworthy, and those that should have died were allowed to spread the poison of their weakness through the generations. Their inferior genes diffused throughout the species like dye in water, until its omnipresence rendered it nearly unrecognizable."

Nearly.

Mother would have liked Vanessa. She knew that I was unique. While Mother raised me, she regarded my failure to assimilate into public school culture as a blessing, explaining that I was too special to be understood by ordinary children.

"Tell me about your mother. She sounds tremendously important to you."

"She knew me. She loved me. She died waiting for a kidney transplant." It was all I could manage, and it was more than I had wanted to share, though I felt a foreign need to share more.

"That's terrible. I am so sorry for your loss, Daniel. Was she ill for long?"

"No. The contrast dye administered intravenously to aid her physician in reading a routine colonoscopy accumulated in her kidneys and diminished their function so severely that her creatinine levels were rising by alarming increments each month. Once she was sick enough to see the doctor, the situation was desperate. The kidney that should have saved her went to a man who suffered from PKD." I could not have displayed more vitriol if I had spat the letters.

Vanessa frowned. "I am not familiar with PKD. Why does it make you so angry?"

"PKD is a genetic disorder in which cysts grow within the kidney, replacing organ tissue and decreasing kidney function to the point of failure. He was genetically unfit for survival. Evolution selected him for extinction, but human medicine deemed him fit enough to steal life from my mother.

"My mother was not genetically inferior. She did not have a condition in which one or more of her vital organs destroyed themselves. She was damaged by human medicine, and she could have been restored to nearly perfect health by a transplant, with many productive years to contribute to the species." I was getting too emotional, showing too much of myself, but I was compelled to continue. "She deserved to live; she died because human pity and a misplaced ideal of fairness dictated that an inferior individual deserved a life-saving organ. She died because there was an excess of unfit patients between her and the kidney that would have saved her."

"Do you resent that you could not save her? You must know it wasn't your fault."

"I do not blame myself. She refused my kidney. I offered it repeatedly, insistently. 'I would not trade a year of your life for twenty years of mine,' she told me. 'You are special, mijo. You cannot understand yet, but God has made you to do great things. You will change the world.' She believed it. Now, here I rest, emoting in a coffee house, and my mother is dead."

Death can be a catalyst. I do not know that I will be doing God's work. I do know that I am special. I believe that my mother detected a quality in me that I must now discern for myself. *I will do more than change the world, Mother. I am going to save it.*

Vanessa frowned for some inexplicable reason. "Are you attempting to convince me that vampires and werewolves are real?"

"Monsters are real. They must be. Stories of vampires, werewolves, and other humanoid monsters have been present through millennia of human civilization. Certainly, it is ludicrous to suppose that vampires could spontaneously assume the morphology of a bat, or that werewolves could grow in stature and mass, while inexplicably manifesting fearsome claws and a thick coat of fur. It is not ludicrous, however, to infer that a man exhibiting unbridled ferocity and a ragged appearance could be described as an unnaturally strong and wild beast. Similarly, a killer who moved with uncommon grace and interacted with unnerving guile could be seen as a supernatural being with a gift for disarming its victims' natural defenses and exploiting the resulting vulnerability with metahuman alacrity."

"Okay, but it seems unlikely that even the most intense adrenaline dump would cause someone to see a normal man as a seven-foot wolf, standing on two feet, possessed of superhuman strength." As she spoke, she glanced about the coffeehouse, clearly concerned that we were being overheard. I appreciated her concern for my privacy, but I was ensnared in the momentum of the most engaging conversation I had enjoyed since...Mother?

"How would a deer describe being hunted by a wolf?"

"Terrifying, I'd imagine."

"Yes," I pressed, "but how would that terror manifest upon the deer's memory? Would its epinephrine-addled consciousness construct an accurate representation of the predator? Could such a terrified survivor recall the wolf as being significantly smaller than the deer who fled without reservation from the overwhelming threat at hand? Not likely," I scoffed. "Human memories have proven to exhibit wildly subjective characteristics. It is likely that any human fleeing from a 'werewolf' would exaggerate the details of the encounter, transfiguring the memory to generate a threat that could reasonably elicit the sensation of terror they fled from."

I had delved deeply enough with Vanessa for the day. She would need to be brought along with precise deliberation. I alone knew the secret that those terrified and ignorant souls lacked the vision to perceive: the "monsters" who attacked them had appeared human, but—born of a ferocity and will that defied human understanding—they had become something more. Like me, they had felt the pull to the hunt and had discovered the power in the blood. By partaking of the blood, they stepped beyond the mundanity of the wise man to ascend to the pinnacle befitting the better man. My first attempt at feeding was laborious; I had never eaten raw meat of any sort before, and the knowledge that I was consuming human tissue gave me pause. Through weeks of practice, the blessing of the blood became clear. Sustaining myself on humans further distanced me from them, and I began to yearn for the next hunt. Feeling the power of my quarry flood my veins while consuming a kill led me to crave their blood.

If they existed in legend, and I exist now, certainly other remnants of a *Homo Superior* society may persist. If I could reach out to others like me without exposing myself to human justice, I could join one of these societies. This could be Vanessa's purpose: by publishing my ideas, as she seemed increasingly likely to do, she could advertise my existence to those akin to me. If covens or dens no longer existed, I could help to construct a *Homo Superior* society, one that avoids the pitfalls of its predecessors, namely the in-fighting that apparently plagued relationships between "werewolves" and "vampires," which I perceived to be more of a class struggle than evidence of inter-species competition.

I arrived at the library checkout counter satisfied with the texts I had uncovered to aid my path to predatory supremacy. The librarian, a perpetually unimpressed fixture at the counter, raised an unruly eyebrow at *The Encyclopedia of Animal Predators* and *Ultimate Predatorpedia*. As he handled *Man the Hunted: Primates, Predators and Human Evolution*, he grunted flatly, "This one's a real page turner, ya know. You're lucky it wasn't wait-listed. Can't seem to keep a hot item like this on the shelf."

"I plan to return it swiftly," I assured him, pleased that others shared my enthusiasm for predatory evolution.

"Yeah, you're obviously gonna rip right through this one," he grunted dispassionately. "Are you sure the three books will be enough?"

He raised an interesting point. How could three texts, as engaging as they promised to be, approximate years of practice and ages of evolution? I would need to broaden my search "Please hold these books; I will return momentarily with further research," I blurted to the taxidermized owl peering wearily through his tufted brow.

"You're gonna read more than *this* in two weeks? Good thinking," he snorted. "It would be a shame if you ran out of books and had to interact with another human sometime in the next two weeks."

"Indeed," I nodded to him. I hadn't considered that fortunate side effect of my research. I quickened my pace to the reference section, hopeful that the approaching fortnight of solitude would be as informative as it would be peaceful.

My hunts had become more frequent and more instinctive over the ensuing weeks. In employing a "stalk, chase, kill" tactic, I had removed the guesswork and uncertainty of hunting humans. By defeating my hesitation, I eliminated any pauses in my administration of death that might have allowed guilt or compassion to creep into the ritual.

It occurred to me that my hesitance to nourish myself with my kills may have been borne of my distaste for the humans I was hunting. Certainly, any human tissue was not a fare I yearned for, but the dregs that I victimized could not be a less appetizing meal: raw human tissue garnished in months of accumulated filth. I would have to overcome my misgivings and embrace the exigent nature of the hunt. Certainly, wolves would not refuse to prey upon an unbathed deer.

I would feed. There is power in blood. There must be. Indigenous South and Central American people used human blood in their rituals, believing in the power of human sacrifice. The Bible claims that life exists in the blood, and it goes so far as to forbid the consumption of animal blood. It could be spilled, but not ingested. Why? Surely something must occur when blood is digested. If all I achieved from the consumption of blood was the finality of my journey from *Homo Sapiens* to *Homo Superior*, that was enough. I would claim whatever meager strength resided within the blood of my prey, and I would add it to my own.

The knock on my door startled me. I hadn't entertained a guest since my mother took ill. Peering through the peephole did little to restore my calm. A female police officer, looking disinterested and impatient, sighed and looked about absently as she waited for a response.

"Just—I will be with you in one moment," I managed. *Relax. If they knew, they'd never send a solitary officer.* I steadied my hands as I unlocked and opened the door. "Good afternoon, officer. How can I help you?"

"Hello," her rehearsed smile was pleasant. "Are you Mr. Acosta?" As I nodded my assent, she continued, "May I come inside?"

I frowned. "Is it entirely necessary for you to come inside?"

It was her turn to frown. "Is there any reason that you wouldn't want me to come inside?"

The entitlement that appeared to accompany her badge irritated me. "There could be numerous reasons. As I did not invite you here, my quarters could be in disarray. I could be in the middle of folding laundry and the idea of an unfamiliar visitor seeing my undergarments could give me pause. The reason is not important, is it? As an innocent citizen, I am not compelled to allow you into my home."

"Mr. Acosta, I don't wish to offend you, but I would like to speak with you in your home to protect your privacy."

I fought the impulse to sneer. "That is certainly a thoughtful consideration on your part officer, but I have nothing to hide from—or share with—my neighbors. We occupy adjacent space, but we do not interact socially. Their perception of me could not inflict a discernable outcome on my existence."

She raised an eyebrow. "You talk differently than most guys around here, Mr. Acosta. Suit yourself, though," she said, shrugging, "we can do this in the hallway." She backed away from the doorway and settled into her interview posture. "There have been some violent crimes in this neighborhood. Have you noticed anything out of the ordinary?"

"Violent crime is disturbingly ordinary in this neighborhood. Everything I've noticed recently is ordinary here. I have seen menacing young men and drug-abusing prostitutes on the sidewalk, increasingly wary shop owners, and accumulations of filth on the streets and alleyways. I do not speak with anyone here, so I have not heard any rumors."

She made a couple of notes, then analyzed my face quizzically. "Aren't you from this neighborhood? Why do you talk like that?"

Curled lip, raised eyebrow: she was judging me.

The idea was so preposterous that I burned to ridicule her, to allow her to wallow in the absurdity of assuming that any portion of her human existence could make her superior to me.

Calm.

As the more mature (certainly more evolved) party, I felt a responsibility to educate, rather than chastise, for all of the good that it might do.

"I speak as I do because the English language was not designed to be broken up into conjunctions and colloquialisms. It was not created to satisfy the accelerated pace of our distracted and self-important existence."

"'Self-important existence?' Such a smooth talker. You *really* must get all the ladies."

I frowned. I had not done anything to attempt to woo her. It was therefore odd that she felt drawn to me. It stood to reason that my growing predatory instincts would project a degree of animal magnetism that human females would find alluring. This presented an alarming and unforeseen development. I would have to negotiate my way free of this predicament, and seek to obscure my primal allure, in pursuit of a less visible profile. "I do not exert myself to gain female attention. I find the concept of romantic entanglement exhausting and, frankly, extraneous outside of reproductive efforts."

"Ohhhhhhhhhhh-kay." She appeared to manage her disappointment well, raising her eyebrows and nodding silently to herself, clearly resigned that I would not return her affections.

Seeking an opportunity to expedite the conclusion of this discourse, I prodded her forward, "If you have regained your professional composure, might we proceed?"

"*See?*" She shook her head. "You talk like it's two hundred years ago."

"There is elegance within the English language," I explained as calmly as possible. "Within each conversation, we preserve its beauty, or we advance its degradation. I choose beauty."

If she responded, I paid no heed. The remainder of the conversation was of no importance to me. I had given her the option to consider a more graceful, sophisticated existence for herself. What she did with that opportunity was largely irrelevant to me. We exchanged mundane pleasantries, and I tacitly agreed to contact her if I saw or heard anything of note. I closed the door, and she was gone.

It was foolish of me to let her bother me. I should have allowed myself to mix blandly into the rest of her interviews. She would remember our exchange.

Foolish. She didn't matter. She was meat.

* * *

I met with Vanessa again. The visits had become regular events over the last several weeks, and upon her suggestion, we had begun meeting more privately. I proposed meeting at Vanessa's home or mine, but she asserted that meeting under those conditions would be unprofessional. As a compromise, we scheduled time in a private work room at the library.

This discussion was more laborious than most, as I struggled to remain focused on our conversation. I felt increasingly out of place amongst humans, who marched so obediently within their daily routines, resembling sheep more than the pinnacle of evolution they professed themselves to be. In the daylight, when the sheep were on the move, their civilization weighed upon me like a leaden blanket. It would be so easy to forget that I was not one of them. I must vigilantly resist the temptation to join the herd, to let its movements become my own, to let its leanings rob me of choice and purpose. As the sun fades, the distractions retreat with the light. With the fall of night, I find clarity.

"People mistakenly claim that darkness obscures vision. This, of course, is an embarrassing simplification meant to keep the timid recessed within their safe spaces while the safety of daylight is removed. While one cannot see as far at night, one can perceive more truth. The daylight is a tame play space with cushions covering all the sharp edges. The night is raw and wild, where the whispers of forgotten instinct can be heard. In the darkness, I know what I've done. I know all at once who I am."

"Who are you?" she said at last. No fear. No hesitation.

This one might understand.

She may in fact possess the vision to see beyond the apparent absurdity of my intent. She undoubtedly acknowledged the absence of fevered madness in me. Could she discern the mercy driving my resolve?

Tell her.

"I am *Homo Superior.* I thin the herd. I save a race that lacks the strength of will to cast aside the weak, old and helpless to move forward stronger, healthier, and more fit for survival. My will, my ferocity, my *instinct* will save your world."

Tonight's hunt would be simple. I had scouted him for days. He was homeless, jobless, and addicted to drugs. He was too old to rehabilitate and too isolated to be missed. Vanessa agreed that, by my accounting of his routine, he had nothing of substance to offer human society. Vanessa was becoming more comfortable with our discussions, sympathetic even. She did not shy away when I, for the first time, disclosed details of my plan for this hunt. She may in time reveal herself to be a kindred spirit, a trusted agent. She clearly perceived me as a son, the ideal son, really. She was too old to learn to hunt, but she could prove her worth by reaching out to her readers with my vision, once she could comprehensively grasp it...

When my quarry crossed in front of my position, I would follow at a distance until he entered the alley to bed down. His routine was consistent. I would wait until I entered the alley to brandish the knife and burst into pursuit, eliciting his flight response while plunging him deeper into the secluded dangers of the darkness between buildings. I would slash at his right hip to keep him to the left and force him to the chain-link fence separating blocks. When he attempted to ascend the fence, I would move for the kill. My confidence had grown with my evolving tactics and merciless prowess.

My eyes narrowed as I saw him exit the shelter a block away and stagger in my direction. It was disgusting that unproductive vagrants could afford chemical diversions. I felt my pulse quicken when he passed in front of me, and I entered into casual pursuit. As expected, he continued to make his way down the street toward his familiar alleyway.

What's this?

He was walking faster, and his limp was less discernable. I quickened my pace to match. Was he alerted? Was he alarmed? Had I somehow betrayed my intent?

Relax. The night was bitterly cold. He may simply seek to bed down in his trash lair and generate some warmth under the insulation.

He moved more nimbly than I would have expected. I could hardly detect his limp when he turned into the alley. This man may have been a poor selection as a prey item. His age was apparent on his face, but he now appeared to be neither weak nor particularly vulnerable. What to do? Break pursuit and scout more suitable quarry?

No. Take him now. He may be more challenging than my typical target, but he remains incapable of posing a threat to me. I have grown fierce. He would not evade me; he would not survive me.

Was this pride? Had I succumbed to such a base and entirely human weakness?

No. Not pride: PURPOSE. I had marked him to die, and so he must.

My supremacy was in its infancy. Could it afford so significant a setback as a failure to hunt?

With the pursuit moving deeper into the alley, I now struggled to casually match his pace. He ducked sharply around the next corner.

Catch him! KILL HIM NOW!

I heard his feet skidding to a halt as I rounded the corner.

Good! The fence has stopped him! The trap is still working!

He whirled to face me as I entered the kill zone. Something was wrong with his face. The old visage of my intended prey was no longer apparent. A disguise! My muscles tensed to spring as he reached into his coat. A weapon? No, a badge. Now, a badge and a gun.

"Drop the weapon!" he called out. "Lay down on your

stomach!" He sounded out of breath and anxious. I would have sworn I could feel his pulse hammering through his arteries from where I crouched several feet away.

My eyes darted frenetically around the alley. I could have run, but I was fatigued by the pursuit. Panting, I gauged the distance between us.

I can make it.

I couldn't reach him before he fired.

He'll miss.

Panic could hinder his aim, but I would need to inspire panic through action.

NOW!

I sprang, blade extended, straining to reach his femoral artery before he could fire. Thunder rolled sharply over me as pain ripped through my thigh. I gasped for air, blinking feverishly to clear my vision. My leg was unnaturally hot. I snapped my head up to see him standing over me, fumbling with handcuffs.

SEE? He wants to capture, not kill. He lacks the capacity to kill. He is inferior. I am SUPERIOR. He has to die now!

A deep growl made its way up my throat as I leapt again, hindered by my thigh wound but tantalizingly close now. CRACK! CRACKACKACKACKACKACK! My body lurched, free of my will.

Lances of white-hot pain ripped through my chest, back, and abdomen. My deafened ears could barely make out the ringing of my blade as it dropped from my indifferent fingers to clatter against the pavement.

Was I breathing?

I couldn't will my chest to expand. Rolling onto my back and gasping for air did little to help. My coughs lay wet and hot across my face and chest.

Blood. I'm dying. How?

I dimly made out feet and legs running all around me. So many officers. This was a trap. Caught in my own trap.

Humiliating. They were ahead of me and behind me. They knew.

How?

Each blink was growing longer. They ripped my shirt open to apply bandages.

They were going to save me.

Human pity, so predictable. As they assessed and bandaged my wounds with surprising efficacy, I could not help but smile.

Such irony.

Surfacing out of deep water. Dull, unintelligible voices. Rhythmic beeping. A strong odor of bleach. A hospital.

I remained still, eyes closed, taking stock of my body and my surroundings. My arms were restrained at the wrist, tethered to the rails of my bed. Breathing hurt my chest. I was alive, but weak, and their captive.

"Daniel, I can see that you are awake. Can you speak with me?"

Vanessa. Why would she risk so much to be here? How could she have gotten in? Was she here to free me? Would she be caught? Did she even have a plan? She had gotten this far...

"Daniel, I wanted to be here when you woke up. I know you're disoriented, and I'm sure you must be in a great deal of pain."

Casting aside my unsuccessful attempt to pantomime sleep, I resignedly cracked open my eyes to meet hers. The room was painfully bright, but I held her gaze. Beyond her, I spotted bars in the windows.

Prison hospital.

I wanted to weep, to burst forth from my bonds and claw my way out of human custody. I knew I was too weak to escape, and who could predict what would happen to Vanessa in the scrum, even if I could pry my hands from their restraints.

"Oh, don't look at me like that, Daniel. This isn't the end

of your story. You are still young; you're still alive."

I gulped against a laryngeal prominence that seemed to have doubled in size. "I don't belong here. I must fulfill my purpose...we shared a purpose," I croaked in a voice that had undoubtedly gone unused for days.

She tilted her head toward me and smiled meekly.

Pity?

"Things don't always go the way we plan. You really are a sweet boy. You'll be safe here. They will keep you out of trouble and get you the help you need."

Why was she was patronizing me?

"I do not require help, Vanessa. What I require is freedom. You heard my reasoning. You agreed with my assertions. How—"

"Daniel, I agree that the human population is probably growing too quickly, and I am aware that you put a lot of thought into your beliefs, but murder was never an appropriate solution. People died. *You* almost died. You isolated yourself from the world, pitting yourself against everyone in it, all of us. You are a young man, a *human*, Daniel, and you need to learn how to exist as one."

She paused, evidently studying the floor with great intent. "You were so obsessed with the changes you felt taking place within yourself, with the evolution of *Homo Superior*, that you neglected a basic fact."

Her visage hardened as she exhaled a breath I hadn't noticed her holding. Standing to leave, she turned her head in my direction once more, and her countenance had changed, her resolute expression softening to pity. "As predators evolve, so must the prey."

RIKKI DON'T LOSE THAT NUMBER
Richie Narvaez

"Hello. It's me. It's Rikki."

These are the first words, the first time, over a long bridge of years, he has heard this voice from his past. A voice like Miles's trumpet, all brilliance and brashness, a little sadness, a voice swirling with exotic ports of call, cherry-topped by nicotine. It gives him an instant erection. Almost instant. He is not as young as he used to be. Plus, there are the drugs.

"Oh my God" is all he can think to say at first. "Rikki? Is it really you?" He wants instantly to know where she is, if she's near. "Are you in town? Tell me you're in town."

"For a little while, yeah."

"We have to get together. We must!"

"That's why I'm calling."

Hearing her voice, the years reel in and he remembers himself as a scrawny, scrubby-faced grad student with a permanent erection, especially for his Neoclassical Lit professor's young wife. The professor liked to host parties at his bungalow overlooking the Hudson. All the lit majors were there, as well as theater, fine arts, music. Rikki stood there that time in the garden, the daffodils rioting at her feet, framed against sunset on the Catskills and the sparkling river. It took him a long time to settle on how he would describe her skin color: he settled on peanut-butter brown. Her hair was a jet-black wavy mess cut in bangs above her eyes. He gravitated toward her not just because she was smoking hot, but also because he had watched her, saw that she took shit from no one. And even when she dismissed his come-ons with brutal condescension, it only urged him onward. And upward.

They talked for three hours as the sun went down. A perfect bubble of time. But when everyone else retired to the fireplace in the den, she moved to go, too.

He grabbed her arm, wrote down the phone number to his parents' house, where he was living at the time, and begged her not to lose it. She smirked as she took it.

Through the filthy cumulus of memory, he can see her still. She has been on his mind the whole time, through three marriages, through hundreds of groupies, through the orgies. He had moved away, at first by choice. But now, he is back, clearing out his some-people-might-call-it-large parents' house, both now dead (cancer, heartbreak), and Rikki is back too, from outer space, or may as well have been. What a coincidence, what a stroke of fate.

She tells him to meet her at La Goulue Gallery in an hour and does he know where it is. He says, "Yes, the old bakery. Then we could go out driving—" but she has hung up. Still he smiles, the kind of smile that almost makes half your face fall off. He knows this is destiny, this is kismet.

He makes time to do twenty push-ups, seven and a half crunches, trim his pubic hair, shit, shave, and shower, and then he realizes he is still twenty minutes early. He sits in his brand-new 1999 Taladro Executive Class SUV, listening to Coltrane for thirty minutes more, so as not to look not cool.

La Goulue seems small at first but widens the deeper he enters. Of the artwork, he is not impressed. A series of pit bulls made of umbrella parts. A vat of neon blue spaghetti. He finds himself in front of a large pen and ink by someone named Motley. It's of two women reclining, nude and intertwined, called *The Babylon Sisters.*

"I knew this one would get your attention."

Ah. There is the voice.

He turns and it's her, out of the past, looking stunning, looking gorgeous, smelling fucking amazing. It's oleander, he thinks. Her hair is wild now, and for a second—and he feels bad about thinking this—she seems darker than he remembers, not peanut butter, and her lips seem a little thicker. And had she been taller before? He thought she had been taller. But it has been thirty years, more, and memory is a tricky, dirty thing, besides the painkillers, sleeping pills, antipsychotics, not to mention hallucinogens enjoyed along the way, of course, and those almost daily sessions of electroshock therapy one winter. Or two.

She embraces him, and he is surrounded by the warmth of her skin and whatever arousing oleander perfume she's got on. *Eau de Viagra,* feels like. She steps back and looks at him, sees something on his face—disappointment? expectation? craving?—so she leans in and kisses him on the cheek. *Wetly.* He flushes in joy.

"It's been so long," he says. "I always knew you would call. So, are you—?"

"You seem to be doing very well for yourself. I hear your band is recording a greatest hits album."

"Uh, really just re-recording acoustic versions of our back catalog."

"How great for you. Everyone's doing that nowadays."

"Are they? It pays the bills, you know. But you, Rikki, you look absolutely stunning." He is about to ask if she remembers

"Slow Hand Row" when she grabs his arm and spins him around.

"There is a man approaching us with a big red beard," she says. "Do me a favor, whatever I say. Just go along with it. It's a business thing. I'll explain later. Over drinks." He is about to object but he likes the way she is grabbing his arm. He can feel her long nails digging in and it warms his crotch like a sun spreading across a rickety porch.

A large bald man with a ferociously notice-worthy red beard inserts himself between them. "Rikki! There you are!"

"Major!"

They air kiss, and she says, "This is Jay, and this is *The Babylon Sisters* I've been telling you so much about."

Major ignores Jay and looks at the pen and ink. "Magnificent. Erotic. I find Motley's work can be called 'art' without implying an insult."

"Nice to meet you, too," Jay says.

"Oh, yes, yes, I've heard your name," Major says, with a chuckle. "I'd recognize you anywhere. I loved most of your first album. Very credible work. Very credible."

"You did? Well, I guess I'm supposed to say 'Thanks.'"

"My card, sir."

The card reads "Major Dude" and has a phone number. Jay is not sure what to do with it, so he puts it in his wallet to get it out of his hands.

"So you co-own *The Babylon Sisters*?" Major says.

Jay's eyebrows fly up. Rikki gives him a look, so he says, "Well, uh, yeah, I do."

"Your bona fides speak for themselves," Major says. "Soon each of us will own a sister, it seems." He turns to Rikki. "I assume we can proceed with the agreed amount."

"Major, sorry, no, it's six now."

"Six! Hmm, still doable. May we conclude our business immediately?"

Rikki turns to Jay and says, "I'm so sorry I have to leave,

but I really have to finish this deal. I promised."

"That's okay."

"Let's meet for drinks tonight. Eight o'clock. At my hotel. I'm at the at the Beekman Arms."

He stands there, with the warmth of her skin and the scent of her still clinging to him like a new pair of leather pants. *Tonight* it is, then.

His dead parents' room is spacious and clean, but he cannot sleep there. Not because it smells a little like death and a truckload of Ben Gay. But because it still feels like an intrusion. Instead he has been sleeping in his old bedroom.

It would have been nice if, like in some movie or sitcom, his parents preserved his old room the same way he left it so long ago. That would have been sentimental and kind of sad, but he could deal with that. Or if they had done the eighty-is-the-new-seventy thing and retrofitted his room into a home gym. That would have been charming in an "aren't old people hilarious?" way. But no, when he first opened the door it looked as if, in fits and spurts, they put some of his stuff into boxes, moved in old lawn furniture, broken lamps, and four cat litter boxes. He squeezed past those and found his old bed, dusty, soft as Jell-O pudding. On it were old toys, his Howdy Doody record player, his Space Patrol car in its original box, a Pet Rock, none of which he remembers owning, but which he must have. He tossed them on the floor at first, but they are now placed neatly on his old toy chest.

He is fetal on his old bed. He considers taking a Valium to relax. But it doesn't go well with his other pills and he doesn't want to get groggy.

He thinks about Rikki, about the curves of her gypsy body, the way she smelled. He smells his upper arms where she hugged him to see if he can still catch a whiff.

The doorbell rings.

He squeezes past a pair of moldy Adirondack chairs and is downstairs before he realizes he forgot his pants. He considers running back up, but instead he grabs a dusty throw from the couch and wraps it around his waist like a fleece sari.

The two men at the door introduce themselves as Detective Ramirez and Detective Massoud. They say they know who he is and just want to ask a few questions.

"I guess O'Hara and Hannigan have the day off," he says.

"What's that?"

"Never mind."

One of the cops says, "I'm a really big fan—I loved your guys' second album. The first side is amazing."

Jay winced. "What about the second side?"

"Yeah, I don't know what you were trying to do there. But I admire that you guys tried."

"Well, I'm going to say 'Thanks.'"

In the living room, they show him a picture of Rikki. It's an old picture, black and white, blurry, from way back then.

"You were seen talking to this woman today," one of them says. Jay is not sure if this is Ramirez or Massoud.

"She's a friend. A good friend. So what? What's the rumpus, as they say?"

"I guess they still say that. Can you tell us what you talked about?"

"She told me she loved our second album. All of it."

"Please. This is important."

He crosses his arm in front of him, and it occurs to him that this is the way he used to sit, on this very couch, when his parents wouldn't let him have extra ice cream. Or was it his first car?

He shrugs. "I can't tell you anything."

"Maybe you're not as smart as I thought you would be. You're the one who wrote the lyrics, right?"

"What is this? What do you want?"

"Your friend—your 'good friend'—appeared in town about

a few days ago. She's never been arrested but she's a suspect in some pretty mean business."

"What kind of business?"

Ramirez and Massoud or Massoud and Ramirez look at each other and nod. "Swindling millionaires," one of them says.

"She gets people to invest in artwork she doesn't own. She has fake papers, gets actors and friends to pretend to be part owners, so that the dupes feel it's okay to invest. Get it?"

Jay says nothing. He has steered clear of the law for many years and doesn't want to get any closer now.

"We don't want you to get caught up in any of this. She could make you an accessory without your even knowing it."

"Is there any way you can help us locate her?"

"No, I just happened to run into her, that's all."

"If you see her again…"

"If I do, I won't tell you a thing."

"Well, here's my card if you have change of heart."

They leave and his nap is ruined and so is the rest of his afternoon.

At eight o'clock he storms into the Beekman. The desk clerk stops him and asks if he can help. He tells them who he is coming to meet.

"In the bar," the clerk says. "Back table."

The bar has a low ceiling, is lined with dark wood, and there are many drinkers and diners, but he keeps his head down, ignores them in case anyone recognizes him, he's not in the mood for autographs or whatever. He keeps his eyes on the back and spies her thick legs before he sees her face. He imagines where those legs go, but tries to change the subject in his mind. He wants to ask her what this is all about, what the deal is with the cops. He walks purposefully, stiffly up to her, stands above her. Oleander.

It's dim in the bar and even dimmer in the back. She is

wearing shades and a turban and a dress now, blue, perfect for a presidential-level stain. He is not going to get distracted. He going to take charge of the situation and not let things get out of hand.

But her perfume has already inched up the legs of his black jeans and tugged him to distraction.

She says, "Please don't mind the glasses. I had to talk to Major for hours, and now I have such a headache."

This throws him off a little. But, dammit, he's still going to see what's what. He's not even going to bring up "Slow Hand Row." At least not right away.

"Listen, it's great to see you," he says. "But I have questions..."

"Sit down. Let's get you a drink."

"Yeah, okay. But I really have to ask you about something." He is taking charge. He. Is. Taking. Charge. "What was that business at the gallery today?"

He sits down across from her and it's then he notices— although he can't be sure—she looks a little bit different than she did that afternoon. He had barely seen her, of course, and it has been so many years. But her ears were different, no? And weren't her breasts bigger? He was sure they were bigger. Maybe it was the outfit. Women can do that, change the look of their breasts with an outfit. It's a big cheat.

"Of course," she says. "Major has money he needs to move around."

Jay knows what that's about. "Hah, you mean to launder?"

"Yes. Everyone does it. I'm sure you have in your time."

Jay nods and a waiter appears and places what looks like a brandy before him.

"What is this stuff?"

"Kirschwasser. It's what I'm having."

The stuff is sweet and a little bitter, with a little more kick than Jay had been planning to have, to keep his head straight. But he doesn't want to get distracted by it. He wants to stay on the subject.

"So he invests in artwork to do so," Rikki says. "Today he bought fifty percent of a painting."

"A painting he thinks I co-own." Aha, now he has her.

"Exactly," she says, as if it's nothing to admit.

"Okay, but...one thing I can't figure out. Major seemed to know I was going to be here, but you had just called me. How did he know?"

"I called him the moment after I called you."

That's not what he meant. He wishes he could see her eyes. Would it be too pushy to ask her to take them off?

"Please," she says, "enough about this boring stuff. Tell me about your newest album."

"Oh, well, talk about boring, no, I don't want to talk about that. Listen, to get back to Major, so you used me to sell that painting for, what, six thousand, six hundred thousand dollars for this guy?"

"Six *million*."

"What?"

"Jay, please don't think I used you. My clients just feel more comfortable if they're investing with people who are well known, people of their kind. You're their kind. I'm not. I owe you. I really do. So drinks are on me. We'll make a whole night of it."

This is what he wants, isn't it, a whole night of it? But her accent—it slips. For a second there it sounded not world-traveled but...New Jersey? The drink. He is starting to get a buzz. "I really shouldn't stay out too long," he says.

"Don't be silly, Jay. It's early. Our wild times have just begun."

He is thinking about what he used to do to women. It was a technique of his own he liked to call "Slow Hand Row."

"Let me take you driving," he would say, doing his best

Bogie. Or was it Gable? He wasn't like other guys, he would say, trying to get to slide home right away, no, that wasn't subtle, that wasn't sensual. "Have you ever seen 'Slow Hand Row'?" Or was it "Slow Hand Road" he used to call it? He's not quite sure anymore.

"Just sit back and relax," he used to say. "You don't have to do a thing. Just watch me." He would whisper how excited he was and then show them what their gorgeous bodies did to him, showing how much they turned. Even past the point of a cramp. It was all for them. It was all about *them*. Even now, probably, even with the arthritis creeping.

He remembers asking Rikki. He remembers, doesn't he? What was it she said? Why does he remember yelling? There should not have been yelling.

He smells his hands. Soap. Where is she anyway?

He is in a hotel room and he does not remember getting there. A strong sun cuts across the colonial-style bed. He is half on, half off the mattress. He does remember that in the middle of the night he had thought to call Major, and now the idea comes again, and he is glad to have remembered it, is proud. He will call Major and tell him the truth, and they will both go to the cops, Rodriguez and Mossad, and they will explain how they had been duped.

Where is she? Did they do it? He goes to the bathroom to piss and he checks himself to see if he had any action at all, and it doesn't look like it. What the hell were they doing all night?

There is no sign of her, only his clothes on the floor. There is a large blue plastic container in front of the bed. Maybe her clothes are in it. He will check, but first he will call Major before she gets back. At bedside, he fishes Major's card from his pants and dials.

A second later, he hears the dull sound of it ringing over his phone. At the same time he hears an echo of the same ring. Is that his hearing again? Years of stupid guitar amps. There it goes again. But it's not coming from the phone.

It's coming from inside the large blue plastic container.

Major must have a mobile phone, but what is it doing in there?

It rings again in his ear and echoes from the large blue plastic container.

What? What the hell?

He goes over to the container and lifts the lid and as the smell of death, of a body that has released its effort to maintain order against the chaos of existence hits him, he easily recognizes Major Dude's head, which rests unnaturally between his ankles.

"Holy shit!"

Knock knock.

"Are you in there, Jay? It's Detective Ramirez and Detective Massoud."

Jay steps toward the door. He will explain everything. They will help him. They will understand. But something stops him. A vague and distant hint of a memory. He foresees terrible trouble.

"We know you're in there," either Detective Ruiz or Detective Masada says. "We have the pass key. We can come in whenever we want."

"What do you want?"

"We know you were with her last night."

He throws the bed covers over the plastic container. He smells the air and realizes the smell of death is all around him. He uses a pillow as a fan.

"Yeah. We're consenting adults." Not that anything happened apparently. "Why are you bothering me?"

"Why don't you open the door and let us help you?"

His instinct decides for him. One shoe left behind, pants half off, like a jerky cam episode of *Cops,* he jumps out the second-floor window, slides down a sloping porch roof, hits the ground hard, sees his SUV parked, and limps fast to get to it.

* * *

He flies down the road, heading he's not sure where, when he notices the note on the dashboard. He reaches for it, one-handed, crumples it just so as he opens it.

"Meet me at the professor's house. At sunset."

It smells like her. But is it her? Is it really Rikki? He just doesn't know anymore. When he thinks of her, he sees a face in his mind, but is it her face or just the face he remembers? Something's not right, something not clicking. It's like a scab that he knows he should leave alone.

He drives to the college, finds a lonely spot past the trees outside Honey Field, waits until the afternoon drains away. Listens to Mingus for hours.

He thought it would be a struggle but he remembers easily where the professor's house is. He parks. The front porch is alive with oleander. The front door is open. From there, he can see straight past the fireplace and to the open back door.

There is a woman waiting there in the garden. Standing in a riot of daffodils.

This one only vaguely looks like the Rikki in his mind.

"Okay. I know you're not her. What do you want from me?"

A voice from behind him says, "How well do you think you knew her?"

He turns and it's the woman from the hotel, the one with the bigger breasts and the lighter skin. She takes off the shades. Her left eye is permanently closed.

"We were friends," he says. "We knew each other for years. Or months, at least."

"No," she says. "You met her for the first time at the party and immediately hung on to her like a child."

"That...that can't be right. I was in love with her."

"You created a scene," says the one standing in the flowers.

"The professor asked you to leave," says another voice. It's the first one, from the gallery.

156

"Your own friends asked you to leave."

"You're lying."

"No, Jay. You kept screaming at her to call you when they dragged you to your car. You screamed your phone number at her, again and again."

They are all talking at him, surrounding him, he has to keep turning his head.

"What do you want from me?"

"Twenty-four hours later Rikki was missing."

"You turned. You ran."

"You sure did. Thirty-six hours later you were in Europe."

"I went there to find myself. To find music."

"Three weeks later they found her body. Her head bashed in with a rock. And she was strangled."

"There was never enough evidence to bring you in."

"You were too well protected. Family money. You stayed away for years, always out of the reach of the law."

The sun above the Hudson was a brilliant blue red orange.

"At some point, you found time to join a band, make some albums."

"Ha! My agent said it would be a disaster," he says. "We proved him wrong."

"Touring all over the world, except for the U.S. Never coming back here."

"At the same time touring a series of mental hospitals, re-habs, and so-called 'health spas.'"

Yeah, that spa where the guru used to say, "Don't put anything in your body that doesn't aggressively want to leave it."

Or did that never happen?

"I had a wee problem with reality," he says. "It's what the third album is all about. Was supposed to be about. It's unreleased. Wait, you were waiting for me to come back? You set this up. This trap."

"Yes, we've been waiting. It took the death of your parents to finally bring you home."

"You don't have proof of any of this. You're making all of this up. You're lying."

"You are our proof. A little acting and some special effects is helping it get out of your head. All you have to do is remember."

"Look at us."

"Look at us and the memory will come back to you."

"We want to take you to the breaking point. We want you to remember."

Their faces, that garden, the Adirondacks in view, the house, the flowers. It shoots into his head suddenly.

He sees the scene. She was tall, towering above the professor's students, and not just in height. Her personality dominated the room. He wanted her like he'd never wanted anyone before.

After he made a fool of himself, yelling his number at her—"You don't want to call nobody else! Nobody!"

He tells the story to them. "I remember," he says. How he went back that night. The door was open. It was always open. She was in the kitchen, drinking water. He held a rock from the garden, a pet rock. And then, to be sure, slow, strong hands. *Slow Hand Row.* He remembers it all for them. He remembers thousands of sweet goodbyes.

"Is that enough for you, lieutenant?" the women say to a man approaching.

"That's enough for me."

It is Major Dude, alive and well. Behind him are Ramirez, with a gun, and Rassoud, with a gun. "I didn't think this would work," one of them says. "Look at him. He's zoned out."

Major Dude puts cuffs on Jay. He says, "You never had a chance. These women, they had your number."

KID CHARLEMAGNE
Kat Richardson

Bear was busy down in the basement, humming along with the music piped into the darkroom's speakers from the Bang & Olufsen hi-fi. Wasn't he Kid Charlemagne: the Godhead of the Good Trip? Yes, he had taken a short fall from grace, and it had taken time to rebuild his reputation, but he was back now, and he'd learned from his time of trials. The lysergic hydrazine was almost ready and he was pleased with the new process, bitch though it was. One more day...

In the candle-lit isolation of the darkroom, the sound of knocking from upstairs seemed like part of the music. But it came again and again, even after the song was over. Irritated, he left the darkroom and checked the small TV screen that showed the view from the ridiculously obvious security camera over the kitchen door.

There was a girl there. A lanky, tie-dye-wearing, second-generation flower-child. Her face seemed familiar, but he couldn't remember her name. Of course, he was also seeing her in blazing technicolor, in spite of the black-and-white CRT. Fun stuff, lysergamides, though the precursors were killer. He hadn't taken anything before starting work, so he must not have gotten his face mask completely sealed...

He locked the basement door behind himself, hung the

mask on the hook outside, and took the stairs three at a time—thump, thump, thump, like the beat of a kick drum to the stretch of his long legs. If the alkaloid process went bad while he was dealing with the girl, that would be an annoyance, but not earth-shattering. It wasn't impossible to replace and stood no risk of exploding at that stage. He was willing to gamble that he could find out what she wanted and send her on her way before the next stage.

He opened the door to a breeze of hay-scent and river-clatter. He stared at her, the colors of her face warping across irrational spectra under the crappy yellow porch light until she spoke. "Uncle Bear? Don't you remember me?"

The colors settled and sharpened, confirmed red-brown hair and sun-tanned skin. Then the sense of her—the slippery unknown details of *now* overlaid on an earlier, younger version of her—aligned. "Addie Hayes? Little Addie?"

Relief bloomed from her and he could almost see it as a thin, fragrant vapor. "Yeah! I'm so glad you remember. Can I come in? My folks are...umm...planning a long trip and they sent me up here to see you."

"Your folks." Esther and Donald? No...Aster! Aster and Donny. Rich kids from Marin, who'd come to soak up the love in the Haight. Shacked up, hitched up, and moved to a big house that blinked empty windows at the sea. "Weren't they just here?"

Addie looked around, craning over her shoulders as if searching for them. "Today?" she squeaked. "Alone?"

Bear laughed, imagining the wisp of a girl in her long, flowing skirt and Indian blouse with the coy peek-a-boo cleavage giving her hippie parents a stern talking-to for coming to see him without her permission. "Like, a couple weeks ago. They must be...traveling a lot lately. Right?"

Addie glanced around again. Nervous little thing, but then, Merced County was the backside of nowhere and his old wood-and-stone farm house tucked into a bend of the river that trudged and tumbled like a stodgy drunk through the farm fields must have been a far and spooky cry from the white split-level in Corte Madera. "Can't I come inside before the mosquitoes eat us alive?" she asked.

"Oh. Yeah. Sure, sure, sure," he said, and waved her inside. He looked past her as she entered, but saw nothing unusual aside from Addie's rusty convertible sitting in the drive. "I'm a little busy, though, so you'll have to wait a bit before I can get you any...uh...supplies."

"Like, how long?" Addie asked as she turned around in the kitchen, wide-eyed. "I think they were hoping to get some stuff pretty quick."

"Patience," Bear said, closing and locking the door. "Neither magic nor chemistry can be rushed, little chickie. Do you want to come see the kitchen, or would you rather wait up here?"

"Isn't this the kitchen?"

Bear laughed again, shaking his head. "Sweetie, this is the chuckwagon. I mean the *kitchen.*"

Addie swallowed and clasped her hands together, burying them in her skirt. "The *kitchen?* Me? Is it...is it safe?"

"Safe?" Bear stopped in his tracks crossing the old lino floor, and turned around, frowning at what a strange, fey little thing she was. "Of course it's safe. Unless you do something really stupid."

He moved closer to her and peered into her face for a long, slow time, trying to see through her skin to whatever was whirling inside her. Addie drew her shoulders together; her small breasts pressed up a little between her arms while she bit her lip.

Bear understood. "Oh...Oh, baby chickie, aren't you sweet? You've never tripped the light fantastic, have you? Oh my, my, my. Mommy and Daddy've been keeping all the magic for themselves, haven't they?"

Addie shrunk smaller under Bear's happy grin. "I—I don't..."

"No?" He sniffed the air, though the smell had always been there, clinging on her, swirling in her windblown hair and hippie clothes. "Not even a little maryjane? A little nip from Daddy's liquor cabinet when the folks are out? Bit of blow when you're up late, studying? Huh?"

Addie blushed. "Only a little! Just...y'know. Like you said."

Bear put his arm around her shoulder. He knew what this girl needed, what she was and what she wanted that she didn't tell anyone. "C'mon. I'll show you where the magic comes from so you'll know it's all right. The backstage, so to speak. Your folks haven't seen that—hardly anyone sees that. Wonderland."

Addie followed him down the stairs to the basement, her small light steps—tssah, tssah, tssah—like the tap of a drumstick on the edge of a snare. She gasped at the clean whiteness of the lab and Bear liked the way the sound bounced around among the flasks and retorts like the fuzzy rainbow crackle of a guitar amp warming up. His hi-fi's sound was never so pure with wonder.

She started walking around the edge of the room. "Wow. All this equipment. It's so...Mad Scientist." She reached for one of the empty flasks waiting on an unlit burner, but pulled her hand back an instant before Bear caught her wrist. She flinched. "Sorry. I didn't know it was dangerous."

"It's not dangerous—it's just glassware. But it's clean and if you touch it, it won't be." He forced an apologetic shrug. "You could say I'm uptight about that kind of thing."

"After all those hippie concerts and stuff, you've got a thing about *dirt?*"

"Hey, I like a little good, clean dirtiness. But contamination is a no-no."

"Oh." She stood in place, turning slowly, staring all

around and bobbing her head. She looked like a heron, all twig limbs and long, drooping feathers. "That's cool. That's cool...but, where's the...umm...the..."

"Passport to a higher consciousness? In transit, you could say." He felt like giggling, which wasn't his thing usually, but Addie looked so adorably Alice in his white-tile Wonderland. Did that make him the White Rabbit? He started singing Grace Slick's lyrics, watching the waves of Addie's hair rebounding off the shore of her shoulders. She was adorable. So very, very...He leaned toward her. "How old are you, Addie?"

"Eighteen." Her tone was defiant, but her eyes were much too large and baby-blue.

He took a step away, frowning. The ergotamine had definitely gotten past the seals and the methodical, math-genius parts of his brain was not at all happy about it. Something didn't add up. "I don't think so. I may be trippin', but I'm not so far gone that I can't calculate. You were knee high when we first met. If you're really eighteen now, you'd have been a lot taller, back in the day."

He leaned down, peering at the enigma. She bit her lower lip—not a sexy Monroe-esque bite, but a nervous, word-holding bite—and hugged her torso, exuding burnt-orange fear. Her breasts rose high into the low scoop of her neckline, revealing a round, black mole. No. A curious little animal nose, shiny black, and hard, hard, hard, sniffing for words. For guilt on which to feed. Nasty creature.

"Little Addie, say again: what brought you all the way out here?"

Addie followed his gaze into her cleavage, then looked up at him with stark eyes and mouthed, "Run."

Bear just blinked as she started walking around the room again, talking. "Well, see...there was this party on the beach, and this guy..." She reached out and touched the nearest flask. Bear started forward, but she turned a warning glare on him. "He offered me a ride to the party, but he's one of those assholes. The 'gas, grass, or ass' kind. You know?" She grabbed hold of the next flask with a double-handed grip like she was going to strangle it. He could clean it later; for the moment, he wanted to figure her out and stood still, watching her move around his lab like a wisp of smoke. "So I took the folks' stuff. For the party. And now, I have to replace it, or they're gonna freak out. Understand?"

Bear squinted at her, the light seeming too bright as Addie seemed to grow darker, but he said, "Yeah, I guess. So this is the guy's idea?"

Addie brightened. "Yeah! Yeah. It was Steve's idea. Tried to get me to, like, lie down and take it. You know? So I stole his car—it's such a piece of shit I didn't even take the keys out of the ignition, 'cause no one would want to steal it—and drove up here."

"So, Steve is your boyfriend." That didn't seem right, but he was trying to put a finger on what was bugging him, and said whatever first came into his head.

"No!" Addie faked silent barfing, and shook her head with a revolted sneer. "Just a guy from the scene. Big black guy." She put her hand up high, as if measuring the invisible man's height, then both hands wide on phantom shoulders, lifting her eyebrows like she expected Bear to recognize the man who wasn't there. "Burn scar on one cheek, real pushy. His buddies call him Moore. You must know him. He knows you."

A small shock ran up Bear's spine, but he shook his head anyway. "Not ringing a bell…"

She stared at Bear, nervous and shivering-scared. "C'mon! If I don't bring something back, he's gonna be really pissed off. And my folks too. Big trouble. You know?"

"So your Steve sent you out here." Bear had an unpleasant, bile-tinged recollection of one Special Agent Stephen Moore from the first time the FBI had tried to trip him up years ago. They lost that case and he'd been back in business in a week. Acid was legal then. The loophole he'd slid through was closed now, and all the shrinks, the Timothy Leary slogans, and the Ken Kesey electric Kool-Aid dreams in the universe weren't going to change that. They certainly hadn't saved his ass down in New Orleans. He snarled at the thought.

Addie went pale, her expression pleading, and a little panicked. "Yeah. For the magic. You and the magic. Still a big deal." Her mouth formed the words "run, run, run" but no sound coming out. "I really, really don't want to cause you any trouble, Uncle Bear..." she said aloud.

Trouble in the shape of another trip to the federal slam. He'd gotten off with eighteen months when the feds had caught him at that festival in New Orleans—they couldn't prove he'd made the stuff, or that he was selling it—but things had changed. They'd pile on everything they could, this time, just for spite. There'd be no way out. No light sentence, no dismissal on a technicality. If the feebs came busting in and found the dark room full of blooming ergotamine, found the hydrazine, the chloroform, and the rest of it, he'd be locked in with animals until they tore him to pieces...He had to get rid of it. All of it. Now!

He wheeled for the dark room door, yanking it open and flipping on the overhead lights. How fast would ergot decompose at this stage? Not fast enough.

Then Addie swept the rack of test tubes off the counter. They crashed down and she yelled, "Oh, I'm so sorry!" Then the nearest flask went toppling as she spun around with her arms outstretched.

"Careful! The solvents in that cabinet are flammable!" He lunged for her, in spite of the fact that she wasn't anywhere near the cabinet. She looked so little, so...fragile as the glassware. Tangled in the colored streamers of confusion, fear, defiance, need...

She pushed him away, screaming, "Run!" and dashed down the row of equipment, throwing it down. The shattering sounds ripped through the cool, white room, rending the peaceful air in jagged red bolts of deceit and fury. "Oh crap, oh crap!" she yelled, standing between the rows and watching him with a solemn face as she threw another flask deliberately on the floor. "Run! Run before it catches on fire!"

He ran. He snatched his kit bag from under the stairs and bailed down the trap door beneath it.

Addie's screams and the sounds of destruction continued until the trap door slammed shut above him. She'd kicked it closed. Alice had dropped the White Rabbit down the hole this time. But this tunnel ran away from Wonderland, out to the old barn beside the river.

The panic colors streaked down the earthen walls around him as he ran for his life. Ran until he popped out at the riverbank and dared to peek back at his little house, bright in the flashing light from the trucks and the cars that tore up his yard. Wavering under the moving shadows of guys in dark, nylon jackets with yellow letters on the back: FBI, Sheriff. Pouring into his house like a dirty flood.

Addie felt fuzzy-headed, silly, and panicked, and weirdly stretched as she bolted back up the basement stairs to the kitchen. Moore and his goons kicked in the kitchen and front doors at the same time, pulling a startled scream out of Addie. And behind it came a giggle she hadn't intended. She hadn't touched anything but the flasks and racks, she hadn't had a drop to drink, and she hadn't had a doobie in hours, but she started giggling anyway.

She was just that happy to have stuck it to The Man in the person of Special Agent Stephen Moore, FBI. Son of a bitch *extraordinaire*.

He brushed past her, shouting for one of the others to hold onto her as he led the charge down the stairs to capture Big Bad Bear. And came back up boiling cold with fury and frustration.

"I'm very disappointed in you, Adeline. The goods down-stairs are ruined and your 'Uncle Bear' has vanished. Looks like there's plenty of other stuff around to use against him, but you understand what's going to happen to you and your folks if I don't find him."

"He ran away. He thought the house was going to catch on fire."

"And left you behind? How'd he get out?"

Addie just kept on giggling as she picked at the little black microphone taped between her boobs. Moore had seemed so scary when he'd caught her after the party, waving the unused blotters of LSD in her face and demanding that she do every-thing he told her to. The bastard with the crappy convertible had turned out to be a fucking narc! She should have guessed he was an establishment stooge—who else would own a car that shitty? Now she'd just stopped caring. "I dunno. Maybe it's magic," she said. "We are in Wonderland, after all."

Moore grabbed Addie by the upper arm and yanked her to a corner of the room; all the better to loom over her. "Where the hell is he?" he demanded.

"I. Don't. Know. He vanished. *Poof!* Like a ghost."

"Don't fuck with me. Possession and transportation of nar-cotics with intent to sell isn't a Sunday-school sin, little girl."

Addie snickered. "Up yours, pig. I'm a minor. Max nineteen months in juvie—you have to let me go when I turn eighteen."

"Your parents are going to be in just as much trouble as you, since they let you get at their stash. How do you feel about that, smartass?"

"It was my stuff. They didn't even know about it. Every-thing I told Uncle Bear was a lie. You can't go after my folks for it. My stuff. My crime. And you can't do dick to me."

"Oh, you're already a jailhouse lawyer, are you? Then I guess you've heard of automatic transfer. No? That's the legal term for when we prosecute minors who commit major crimes as adults. You made your deal with me on your own, as an adult, so when you broke it, you take the consequences like an adult. No bullshit. So tell me where to find Bear, or you're going to be doing some very hard time with some very rough customers, Miss Adeline Hayes who says her parents weren't holding enough LSD to trip out half of Marin County. Want to change your tune now?"

Addie did not. But she thought about it a lot for the next sixteen years. And eight more after that.

The radio played "Radar Love." Adeline snorted at the lyrics and rammed the Mustang's accelerator to the floor. Warm prairie wind poured over her hair as the convertible ripped through the night, away from the beautiful glow of the city, and into the star-spangled midwestern dark.

Songs weren't the only thing that could be forgotten out here. It had been a long while since she'd last seen Bear—and that had been at a distance. She needed him to remember that he was the Once-and-Future King of the Counter Culture's Kool-Aid. And, hell, if he couldn't, she would remind him.

Unlike the music and the man, the road she was flying down had all the personality of a mayonnaise sandwich. Adeline thanked God for caffeine and all forms of speed that kept the boredom from sending her and the rental into a ditch in the course of the four-hour drive. She could hardly tell a difference between the place she'd gotten on the highway and where she got off it. *Christ, Bear,* she thought. *You sure found the backside of Bumfuck.*

After another hour of driving smaller roads that all looked exactly alike to her, Addie finally found Bear's place. It was a far cry from the old ranch house: a lost adobe sugar cube on the golden grain fields that stretched as far as she could see, secluded and undisturbed, except for the distant passing of trucks on the black thread of highway two miles to the south. The sun was barely up and the air was already getting warm and sticky.

The radio in the convertible vamped out the piano solo of "People Are Strange" by the Doors as she pulled into the gravel driveway. She was windblown and tired and she figured, yeah, they didn't come much stranger or more wicked. She looked in the rearview mirror to untangle her hair with her fingers, and scowled at the way the early morning sun highlighted the wrinkles around her eyes. God, forty sucked.

The front door opened as she swung out of the car, all long legs and short business skirt.

"Adeline Hayes." Bear had become thinner, grayer, and though he still stood straight, he seemed worn down now. Old as she had not imagined he could be. Maybe she'd retained her juvenile image of him—tall and athletic and stuck in the seventies, long hair, bellbottom jeans, and all—thirty forever. At least she still looked better than he did—not that she had a choice in an industry where men could get away with any damned thing, while a woman was a has-been the minute she wasn't both prettier and a smarter shark than her peers.

She smiled and waved as she walked to the tiny porch with its long, log-ended overhang. "You remember me after all this time."

He didn't smile back. "I'm not likely to forget. You shouldn't have come here, but I suppose there's no point in asking how you found me, or in turning you away, so you might as well come inside."

She ducked past him, just as she had the first time. Bear closed the door behind them, locking in the cool dry air that tried to escape into the heat outside. The interior was spare: dark floorboards, white plaster walls, furniture that remembered when it had been part of a tree. "I don't suppose I could get a drink, could I?"

"Water?"

"Something stronger?"

"Coffee's the strongest thing I've got."

She offered a bemused expression. "Really? Kid Charlemagne hasn't got a glass of wine or a bottle of tequila around?"

Bear scowled. "I don't do any of that anymore. I'm a solid citizen, unkinked my life, got married..."

"No kids?"

He flicked a dismissive hand her direction. "I've screwed up enough kids without having to raise any myself. If the old product is what you came for, you're out of luck."

"You were the producer of the cleanest acid of the psychedelic scene, the purveyor of the perfect trip for a generation and more and you just...quit?"

"Twice in jail, on the feds' radar no matter how clean I live. Changing names and homes every time someone looks at me sideways. The Man never forgets or forgives, and no matter how much time you do, no matter how far you stay from it, he's always looking for the moment you trip up."

"Or trip out?"

Bear gave a reluctant nod. "That too. It got so every time I dropped any, all I ever saw were monsters. The trip is only as good as your own mind lets it be. No matter how clean the product. Paranoia will kill you."

Addie cocked her head, speculating. "How long's it been since you cooked anything up?"

Bear studied her for a minute or so before he replied. "You still on Moore's hook?"

"No. I work for a tech company outside San Jose. About six years now. I got a surprisingly good education in jail—gives you some time to study."

"They should have gone easy on you. You were just a kid."

"Was. But Moore didn't really care. He hated you, you know."

"No shit. What about you?"

She shrugged and started unbuttoning her blouse. "I don't take after Agent Moore. I am not a cop. I'm not working for any police or law enforcement agency, or anything else like that." She pulled the blouse open and stood up, turning around so he could see her nearly-bare torso. "No wire, no mic…"

"They're not as big as they used to be."

Addie glanced down at her tits. "I think they've gotten a little bigger."

"Christ. That's not what I meant. Bugs aren't as big as they used to be—thanks to companies like yours. All that wire and tape's just Hollywood bullshit now."

"You can put my clothes in the freezer, if that's what it takes to convince you I'm here on my own hook. Put my purse on the front porch if you want—it's not like anyone's going to come around and steal it. I'm not here to trap you into anything. I'm just here to get the recipe."

Bear goggled at her. "What? Why?"

Addie continued calmly undressing. "It's the new thing in the tech business. Creative edge. Drop a micro dose and the ideas just flow like water. So they say. I wouldn't know—I'm in procurement, not design. I just need to keep the clever little boys happy."

"Jesus!" Bear grabbed a knitted throw off the nearest couch and tossed it at her. "Stop that. Cover up."

Addie ignored the blanket, letting it fall as she kicked off her shoes and dropped her clothes on the floor. "What? Afraid the wife will see me standing in your living room bare-assed?"

"She's out of town."

"I know. So what's the problem?"

"You! I said I don't do that anymore. Because of *you*! I'd just gotten back, just gotten my work on track again and you showed up and burned all that to the ground! If Moore had caught me right then, right there, they would have locked me up for the rest of my life!"

Addie folded her arms under her breasts. "I *was* locked up. For sixteen years. You ran and I served in your place. No one fought for me—I had to fight for myself. And I have fought every day to get where I am. So imagine my surprise when I

found out that what I'd gone to jail for could finally be useful
to me. So I came to get it."

"I. Don't. Do. That. Any. More! I don't even remember
how!"

Addie scoffed. "You're a liar, Bear. You wouldn't be afraid
if you had nothing to hide. You still know how to cross the
diamond with the pearl and come up with the cleanest trip
ever to tickle a brain. You couldn't give that up—feeling like
God creating the heavens and the earth. Who could? You are
still Kid Charlemagne."

Bear chewed on the inside of his lip as Addie gave him her
coolest Mona Lisa expression.

"And you owe me," she said.

He stared at her face, silent for a couple of minutes while
Addie just stood there, still bare as a newborn. Finally he let
out a disgusted sigh. "Fine. Get dressed and put on those
boots by the door."

"Why?"

"Because we're taking a long walk."

Addie grinned.

It wasn't a walk, so much as an expedition through the fields
of knee-high wheat—or whatever it was—that rustled against
Addie's bare legs for a couple of miles. Addie's calves were
striped with thin cuts from the long leaves that drooped from
the sturdy stalks, and she was sweating by the time they
reached the old cinderblock shed.

"What's this?" she asked.

"Work shed, and pump house for the irrigation wells,"
Bear said, unlocking the padlocks and easing open the warped
old wooden door. "Technically, it's not on my property, but
the owner's retired and he doesn't mind my using it in exchange for doing a little labor and upkeep at this end of the
field. Get inside, out of the sun, and I'll show you what I've

been working on lately."

She went in as he closed the door behind them. Yellow light crept through the cracks in the door, barely illuminating the shed's interior. The air inside was already hot and thick with must from stacks of moldy straw bales and bins of old grain rife with mouse poop. Bear pointed across the cracked cement floor to a second door—newer and more robust than the first. Addie hurried toward it.

At the next door she stopped and had to wait for him to catch up. Somewhere between the first door and the second, he'd put on a plastic overcoat and carried one of those filter masks that look like some kind of big white bug. "This'll take a minute. Sit down," he added, waving at the nearest stack of bales. Huffing with annoyance, Addie sat and waited, the dirty straw stinging the backs of her abraded legs, while he fiddled with the locks for what felt like five full minutes before he opened the door. He slipped the filter mask over his face as he started to step through, then turned back. "Hang on," he said, muffled by the fiber filter over his nose and mouth. "You'll need one of these. Just in case," he added, fumbling inside the unlit room for another mask, which he handed to her.

It was dark inside until Bear flipped on the lights—first dim red ones, then the full flood of old fluorescent tubes that hummed and flickered as if they hadn't been used in a while. The windowless cement room reminded Addie of the lab in the ranch house's basement without the white tile. But in this case, one end of the room held a row of flat trays she hadn't seen in the old place.

"I recognize the set-up. But what's that?" she asked.

"Rye mold. I'm culturing the ergot myself. Importing lysergic acid monohydrate is tightly controlled now, so I'm synthesizing from scratch. Ergot is the base and, luckily, it grows on ears of wet rye."

"As in rye bread?"

"The grain. About fifty acres of rye out there," he answered, tinkering around with one of the flasks, and a carboy, and an unlit Bunsen burner. "Usually it just gets plowed under to reinvigorate the fields and no one cares if it gets moldy. If you eat it, breathe it, or take it in through the blood, you hallucinate. If you get too much for too long, you get a little crazy, have convulsions, and lose circulation to your fingers and toes until they rot and fall off. There's a theory knocking around that Salem witches and the girls who accused them were suffering from ergotism—out of their minds on the rye mold that had gotten into the grain supply they all ate. Funky shit, huh?"

Addie felt a little dizzy—the lights were really bright and it irritated her. "Was that what I was sitting on out there in the shed? Moldy bales of rye?"

"Walked through it too." Bear set the flask of clear, oily-looking fluid over the burner. "Those bales are feed stock for the synthesis of lysergic acid hydrazine. Isomerize with heat and, when cooled, convert that to LSD by mixing with an appropriate acid and a base. That's where the magic happens—in the choice of acid and base. Then dilute to an appropriate dosage with pure alcohol—not kerosene, like they used up on the hill back in the day—and apply the liquid to a medium like fiber paper or gel—you should be writing this down."

"Shit..." Addie muttered staring down at her scratched and dirty legs.

"Don't get freaky on me yet. Ergot is photo-sensitive." He pointed upward. "It breaks down really fast in strong light."

"So, you just ruined the batch?"

He nodded. "Just like last time. But there are finished blotters in the lock box under the counter—like the ones you stole from your parents."

Addie got up in his ratty face. "Don't get pious with me, Bear. You're the one who made the shit."

Bear remained calm as a windless sea. "And you're the one whose foolishness brought Agent Moore to my lab."

"I also warned you off and took the heat myself."

"That was your choice," he said. "You could have run the same way I did. But now you're here, looking for the door to Wonderland again. Only this time, you're not trying to save anyone's ass, you're just trying to get rich off the ride."

She grabbed onto his plastic overcoat as if to shake him, but he put one elongated hand up between them. "Now, now. Don't get pissy. It's not a problem. You said you wanted the recipe, but it's not that simple. I could show you the process, but you can't sell the trip if you've never taken it."

"You want me to drop acid?"

"You already have. Your mask was soaked in it. With the way you're sweating, we're just waiting for the show to start."

"You rat-fucking bastard."

"You're not going to have any fun with an attitude like that." He shrugged out of her grip and turned to light the Bunsen burner, turning it down low. "Oh, don't tip over this flask by accident—this shit combusts like a motherfucker. Leave it alone and it'll spark off on its own in a couple of hours."

Horror gripped Addie's lungs. She snatched off her mask and stumbled backward. Bear caught her.

He dragged her to a corner near the door and helped her sit down on the floor against the wall. "Don't move fast, and you'll be all right," he said, removing his own mask. "It's a big dose, but it'll wear off in about half an hour. Maybe forty minutes—you are kind of skinny, Addie. You should take better care of yourself."

Bear really did look like a bear, with his big head. His nose was going a bit snouty as she watched. "Oh, God…" she muttered. "How could you do this to me?"

"You didn't give me a lot of choice, little Addie. Remember I said The Man doesn't forget and he doesn't forgive? That applies to both of us. Moore's dogged my heels every day since we met. I tried to live straight, but he wouldn't let me. I'm still an outlaw to him. To all of his kind. And so are you. That's why I'm doing this. Because I have to get out of here and I can't take you along. So listen up. Be careful what you carry. Be careful what you say and who you know. No matter what you do, no matter where you go, he's wise to you, wise to what you are. If you find my notes in the cabinet, they're all yours, but you'll be taking a hell of a risk. Best bet: just crawl away and let this place burn to the ground. Crawl off and be someone new. Someone clean."

Addie was sure she was clean. She was underwater. Wasn't she? She watched his words crystalize and float away from his mouth, like dirty ice. "What," she started, distracted by the way her own voice turned purple and spiky. "What about your wife?" Funny she could breathe underwater...

"Did I say I was married?"

Addie nodded stiffly, watching a razor-sharp fish pop out of an electric outlet and swim across the undulating floor behind Bear.

"I lied. She's just a woman I was shacking up with. She'll be fine. Even if the house burns down. We'll all be fine once I'm out of here. By the way: is there gas in the car?"

"Gas...? In the car?" The fish didn't care about gas or cars. *She* should care, but she was worried about the fire and the fish. Would the fire get her or would the fish eat her...?

"The rental. The convertible."

"Yes. Yes, there's gas in the car."

"Thanks Addie." He bent his big head and kissed her hair. "The world falls apart, but you can get away if you're willing to give it up. I've got to get along now. You take care."

The water closed over her head as the door closed behind him. Then the fish turned, its mouth gaping and full of needle teeth as it swam toward her. It looked very hungry.

THE GIRL COULD BE SO CRUEL
Jim Thomsen

"Donny? Would you come up here? Please? Tonight?"

It took me a few seconds to remember that only one person had ever called me Donny. And that person had disappeared from my life seven years ago.

"Donny?"

"Abby? Holy shit—I mean, hi. I mean, what? Where?" The sample wedding invitations that Thuy asked me to weigh in on, as if I really had any say, slipped from my fingers and all over the kitchen floor of our newly purchased condo.

"Bellingham. Can you come now?"

I dropped into a chair, bumping the last of my Jameson-and-ginger from the arm and dumping it onto the floor and all over the samples. Thuy was going to kill me. But already I'd forgotten about that. Because, Abby.

Abby. The last time I saw Abby was just before I graduated from college.

She didn't. Or wasn't going to, or so I gathered because she hadn't shown up at any classes—or anywhere that I could find—those last two months.

And I looked. Believe me, I looked.

That's what you do for your best friend, right? *Best friend* didn't seem exactly right, even as I formed the thought, because

177

I wished it had been so much more, and it sort of had, for a hot moment. But those were the only words that came.

"Donny?" Her voice softened, deepened, became almost whispery, the way she did sometimes on late nights when it was just the two of us and she was tired, and tired of who she thought she had to be around anyone else. "Are you in?"

Abby had never been much of one for spelling things out. She gave you a little, and if you guessed the rest well enough, or just bought in based on what you could get, you were in. Was I ever in?

For the last seven years, I would not have said yes.

"Wait, what? Tonight? Jesus. I live all the way in—"

"I know. But I need you. I can't say more, not on the phone. In case he comes back."

"He? What?"

A long shuddering breath was her only response. And something in me came unsprung, just a little.

"Abby? Are you okay?"

"You said—" Another tortured breath. "You've always been there for me. Remember? You said you'd always be there for me. Can you be there for me now? Please?"

Hadn't I told her that the last time I saw her? That she could always count on me? The question was, could I count on her? And the answer was, of course not.

But it had never been a reciprocal kind of deal, not completely. Never could be between a schlubby tubby and a sexy Sadie. But, if there's something I know now that I didn't then, it's that love, true love, isn't transactional, and if it is, well, your books never really balance out. It'd be nice if they did, but if they don't, do you ever really close out the account? Not until the overdraft notices pile up a while. And maybe not even then. Not until the sheriff's deputies change the locks on your life and haul away everything inside.

I've spent every day trying to remember that. And to forget Abby. Even after I met Thuy, who sort of marched into my life and took over its management, running all departments of me as efficiently as she did the nursing staff at the hospital where we worked. Which, after Abby, was something I needed. Otherwise, I'd probably still be one of those sad sacks sitting at the end of the day at the end of the bar in some chain restaurant, BJs or Red Robin or TG-fucking-I Fridays, drinking overpriced drinks, trying to catch the an eye at a table full of schoolteachers or secretaries, and hoping my cologne could overcome the "stench of death" that overcomes every single man with a sandblasted heart who hasn't dealt with his shit.

But would there ever really be an "after Abby"?

If I didn't know the answer then, I did now.

"Of course I'll come. I'm in," I told her, and even as I did, I tried to think how I would square it with my fiancée, who was not used to me making decisions without consulting her. Or me making decisions, period. Let alone square it with the head of my pathology lab. Or my bank balance. All of which would be very unhappy with me.

But no matter. Abby needed me.

Would you come. Not could. *Would.*

Ten minutes later, I threw a bag in the trunk and sped off, north, into the rain, into night.

The last time I saw Abby also began with a late-night phone call. And a plea for my help. And of course I went. She'd given me the street address, and even though I'd plugged in the GPS on my phone, it wasn't until I'd circled the Whatcom County Jail three times looking for it that I realized the address *was* the Whatcom County Jail.

It took a while before I was allowed to see her. She looked badly washed out, drained of the primary colors that made her *her,* and not just because of the bleach-stained orange of her jail uniform.

She wept. Told me she couldn't ask anyone else. Not her

wealthy daddy, not any of her daddy's wealthy friends, not "Aleksei," whoever the fuck that was. They'd hold it against her, use it to use her, to bend her over, to break her.

But, she said, she could trust me. "You're my best friend," she said, and that made my heart sing. And sting.

She danced around the details of the arrest. Something about solicitation, or promoting solicitation. Something about an undercover operation, a combined task force, a confidential informant, cocaine located in a Coach purse. She didn't know about any of it, didn't do drugs, she swore. When I looked at her eyes I wondered fleetingly if the redness was merely the product of prodigious tears.

I'd never known Abby to do drugs. But what I didn't really know about Abby would fill a set of World Book Encyclopedias, and I suspected that's the way she preferred it.

But I took Abby on faith, because Abby was my religion.

I struggled to get the gist of it as she spilled bits of information like broken glass all over the filthy green tile all around us. A lease in her name. A condo just south of the British Columbia border, south of White Rock. White Rock, which even a late-night lab geek like me knew was home to what seemed like half of the strip clubs in the world that weren't in Las Vegas.

And Aleksei, again. Fuck that fucker. I'd stand over his dead body someday if he did this to her. A favorite saying of ours came to mind, something one of us would say anytime we heard about someone dissing one of us: *I'll work the shovel if you hold the flashlight.*

It was something we said a lot because nobody at school understood her and me, and she defended me almost as much as I defended her, and neither of us felt any need to explain what we were and what we were not to anybody else, and that just made more out of the mystery of us to most people.

Which, I had to admit, was more than fine with me, the idea that people had half a crazy idea that the local Jughead was somehow getting to bend his crown between Veronica's legs every time they saw us laughing it up in the Viking Union coffee shop or on the rim of the fountain in Red Square. I didn't fuel the speculation. But maybe I did by not pissing on that particular fire. And maybe I knew that.

Finally, over the jail's visiting-room phone, Abby did say something I understood too clearly. Would I get her out?

It came out after much more dancing that what she needed was money, because any she had, had probably been seized in the raid. A raid which swept up more than two dozen other people, including a port commissioner and a state senator and the XO of the naval air base on Whidbey Island.

It was a scandal, maybe a scandal with serious cable-TV legs. And she couldn't begin to run from it until she could begin to run from the sterile, scuffed gray-green room in which we both sat.

I looked at Abby's face: old, raw, sad, maybe almost fully genuine. Her tears, and I'd never know her to cry. Her fingers as they touched the glass wall between us. As if, maybe, they were desperate to touch mine.

"Can you help me, Donny? It would destroy my father to see me like this."

Think how I feel was the first thing on the tip of my lips. The second, once I got a look at the bail amount, was: *Where did you get the idea that I have that kind of money? That I ever had it? I'm here on partial scholarship, and barely hanging on here with it.*

So of course I said I'd take care of it.

Would you take care of it, she'd said. Not could. *Would.* Because she believed in me, believed that I had what it took to come through. That was enough to ensure I would, whether or not I could.

* * *

I scrambled for the next several sweaty and sleepless hours. Spoke to a bored bail bondsman. Shook awake some friends. Stretched out some already strained friendships. Slipped into my mom's house before dawn and slipped some bills out of her purse. From my stepdad's house, stole a small stash of cash I'd discovered in high school when I discovered his basement pile of Asian porn. Stopped by a few pawnshops with a few items of electronics, some of which were even mine. Shook out a giant jar of loose change I'd been piling up since sophomore year, and rolled every last nickel, dime, quarter and penny by hand. Sprinted to the bank just before it closed to cash in some savings bonds my grandmother took out in my name at a time in my life when girls, even girls like Abby, were still nothing but nothing to me.

By late Saturday, I had it. And as I hauled ass back to the jail, I felt pretty damn heroic.

I would step in. Take over. Take care of her. Take care of this Aleksei fuck, who I pictured as some Eurotrash slickster with disco chains and a shiny fake Versace shirt open to his chest who'd fold like a church-basement chair the minute he was confronted with classic American resolve. She'd see me in a whole new light. Not just as her study buddy or her happy-hour sidekick or her worshipful once-in-a-while shoulder. No longer just the Jughead who, she once said, made her laugh until her balls ached. Now she'd see me as a man. A man who stepped up and took care of shit when it hit the fan blades and flew all over a life. The command-presence kind of man she seemed to care about catering to the most.

Finally, just before sundown, Abby was free, and in my car. I would take her home with me, I told her. We'd be together. I'd handle everything, even though I had nothing left. I said it over and over, every which way I could think of, babbling from sheer exhilarated exhaustion, believing that I could make her believe that I was the strong man she'd been looking for all her life.

She didn't nod. Didn't say anything. For several minutes, didn't do anything. Then she said, "Can you drive out to the lake?" Lake Whatcom, where we'd kayaked sometimes on late spring mornings. There was a dirt road, full of summer cabins, all boarded up and bundled up under a shroud of sodden leaves for the coming winter. There was a gate, but she knew the combination to the lock. Of course she did, and I wondered for only half a second what she did, and who she did, to get it. There was a dock, and a private place to park in front of it.

She put one hand on my leg, high on my thigh, and my bloodstream seemed to heat to one hundred and eighty degrees.

She stared across the lake as the last of the day's gray light started to slip behind the treetops. Then she turned to me with a strange lunar gaze that I decided to see as lust and slowly unbuttoned the top of my pants, then tugged at the zipper. Then at my pockets until I sat up and shot the seat back and let her shrug my pants to my knees, hardly daring to breathe. The air seemed full of glass shattered into dust as she took me in one hand, and lowered her head to my lap.

When she was done—when I was done—she panned me again with that peculiar moonscape face and finally spoke. An address. A safe place, she said. Told me to take her there. Told, not asked. I almost thought to argue, but my will to fight felt as wilted as my erection. I didn't have it in me any longer.

I did what Abby told me to do. Stopped in front of a gate and a keypad, to which she gave me the code in a washed-out whisper. Pulled up to a waterfront condo. Watched as a bedroom curtain twitched and a gray face peered out.

I felt the fine hairs on the back of her hand as she brushed my cheek. She never met my eyes, not even as she stepped out of the car. Her only words, in a voice so small I could barely hear it: "You're my friend."

* * *

She never answered my calls, my texts, my chat messages. Letters in the goddamn U.S. mail, even. They went nowhere, and then they went back to me. Never answered the door of the last address I had for her when I knocked on it five or six times, or was it fifty or sixty? She'd disappeared into some dead-letter office of the heart. Even after the charges against her were dropped. Something about missing evidence, and diplomatic immunity, and missing witnesses they suspected were somewhere in Canada. Again, that sense of forces too big for me to comprehend working in her favor. Like protecting like.

I was angry, but what is anger in the face of love? Anger soon soured into self-pity, and then into curdled sadness, and then into a sallow mist in the back of my mind and the basement of my heart, as I went to work and then somehow *became* work and then somehow met somebody at work who seemed to want to be with me even if she was the one who preferred to be the strong one because, I suspected she more than suspected, I was not. And she wasn't wrong. Abby had taken away the best of me—or had it been thrown away and had I not bothered to look for it?—and Thuy had staked a steel-plated claim on whatever was left. I couldn't say with any clarity. After graduate school, life became a numb blur. I was a lab monkey by day and a neutered housecat by night.

Though, once in a while, on one of my many nights of stark raving wakefulness, often on the couch to which I'd banished myself after one of our egg-timer coital appointments so Thuy could sleep, I wondered if what Abby actually said was, "You *were* my friend."

It seemed that I would never know, and not knowing was a slow death.

As long as I'd known Abby, going back to our freshman year at Western, she'd been vague about the places she called home.

She was always subletting or housesitting or houseguesting,

and those housesits and houseguest situations and sublets were always on some sandy shore, and always from some silver-pompadoured friend of her father's or some well-connected fellow she'd met during her frequently infrequent stints as a restaurant hostess. There was always some comp deal, a gift or a loan, open credit lines and charge cards. Lots of new clothes after long weekends out of town. Nice cars that weren't quite hers and weren't quite not.

I never quite got the full picture between caption-free pictures on social media and captured bits of peripheral chatter when we had the occasional lunch or happy hour. But I soon came to understand that this was how beautiful people lived, on a boundless stream of gold-plated goodwill staked on unstated promises. And that the rest of us were grinders who made do with grubby second rooms in old shitty apartment buildings or, God forbid, shared dorm rooms for half of junior year while trying to work our way off the work-study program, studying bloodborne pathology late into the night almost every night.

But this time I had an address. And I arrived around four in the morning, after a harrowing, headache-inducing drive through a rolling rainstorm up and down Chuckanut, the mountainside drive along north Puget Sound that, on a late fall night like this one, looked more than ever like something out of a sinister 1940s' movie, *Dark Passage* or *Out of the Past*, something like that.

The house was as low-slung and sleek as a sports car—of course it would be sleek, being associated with Abby—and I sat in the drive for a long moment and stared at the half-shuttered moonlight glancing off its acres of glass through a bridal train of trailing mist. I was afraid of what I would betray when I saw her.

I was off-center for another reason, and it took that long moment for it to come to me: Nice or not, late fall in the cold and rain was not an Abby sort of scene. She always said she could stand Bellingham only in July and August. She was a woman of warm summer breezes and wind-snapped spinnakers and seaside nightlife, always disappearing for the few months in the summer or a few weeks in the winter. Or even in the middle of a semester, to St. Barts or St. Maarten or Sagaponack or Sanibel Island, always with some sketchy-sounding job like "club hostess" or "brand ambassador," always with vague stories later about what she was doing and who she was doing it with.

What was she doing here, now?

Somehow she managed to skate by in her classes despite these disappearing acts, and sometimes—okay, more than sometimes—that was with my help. Some of my best memories of college were of her breezing into my place with a bodacious tan and big boxes of takeout teriyaki and a bottle or two of something pretty amazing, and helping her catch up till well past what my mother used to call the test-pattern hour.

Sometimes she'd announce a break in the middle of a calculus problem, and we'd put on music and we'd dance. Badly, hilariously, shamelessly, serendipitously. She'd call out a word or a phrase at random, and I'd make up a dance for it: "Donny! Do The Spatula! Now do The Instant Oatmeal! Now try the Dri-Weave With Wings!"

We'd just about rupture our pancreases laughing as we collapsed onto my big beanbag chair. Sometimes we'd lay there, almost touching, barely breathing, and watch classic movies until the sun came up. She loved them, especially the women: Lizabeth Scott and Barbara Stanwyck and Gene Tierney and Ida Lupino and Veronica Lake. Once we'd gone out to breakfast after an all-night moviethon, arguing the whole way about whether Violet got the shaft in *It's a Wonderful Life*. I told her she took Violet's side because she *was* Violet, and she went silent for a long moment. And then said that I was right.

Of course I'd wanted to kiss her, and of course she knew it. So of course I didn't, because of course I couldn't.

And then the second thing struck me, speaking of things that weren't an Abby kind of scene: that giant gold-flake Escalade parked in front of my ten-year-old Elantra. The Abby I knew liked her rides small and sporty, slightly old-school and European: Porsches and Triumphs and Ferraris, that sort of depressed-heiress thing. Cars she sometimes referred to as sex on wheels or mobile midlife crises. Cars like her father and her father's Cialis-ad pals drove.

This one, I thought, looked like something a Russian mobster in a movie would drive. For the first time in seven years, the name Aleksei shot into my mind. What the fuck was I walking into here?

I opened the car door. It didn't matter. Abby asked, so I came. I was what she needed. What, in her midnight hour, she cried out for.

The pool of blood spread at least fifteen feet in every direction, and had darkened and dried into its own matte-finish floor. It looked weirdly appealing under the warm track lighting, with thousands of tiny seams that looked like the tasteful wire brushing you'd see on high-end stainless-steel surfaces. Sealed within it was a languid fan of long black hair, still lustrous and lightly curled. Like something you'd see on a Michelangelo ceiling.

It was almost mesmerizing enough to overlook the body at its center, frozen in what looked like the middle of a freestyle stroke, and the multitude of bullet holes that ran from its navel to nearly the nape of its neck.

A curl of cigarette smoke slid past my face and snapped me back to the moment.

"Tell me what happened." I turned to Abby, leaning against the kitchen doorway, hand up, fingers out, Salem Light smoldering. Dark circles around her eyes. Give her fifteen pounds and a pair of oversized sunglasses and she'd look like a deliciously depraved Joan Didion.

Seven years hadn't stolen her beauty, but it had hardened

it, sealed it like wood decking for a stormy winter. She was thinner, tighter, shinier. As if her skin had been stretched out to make her seem so taut that she was about to snap. Which, apparently, she already had.

"He loved me," she said. "In his way. As I suppose I did him. In my way. But in his culture the love of a woman and the ownership of a woman are the same thing." She tapped the ash into a wineglass with a brittle snap of her bony fingers. "And nobody owns me. You hear me, Donny? Nobody fucking owns me. He thought me coming back to town to see my father into the ground meant that he—we—could just pick up right where we left off. That I'd be his goddamned squeaky-clean front girl again. That I'd be his girl again, or maybe just one of his goddamned gigaton of them." She lowered her head and looked at me through a more distant version of those lunar eyes I had seen when I had last seen her.

"I didn't know it till just before Daddy died, but Daddy got those bullshit charges not just dropped, but expunged. The last thing he did for me before packing me off like an embarrassing pregnancy in Peyton Place."

"That night at the jail," I breathed.

"Right. Like I was some fucking working girl. I don't mind work, but I'm nobody's working girl."

"I never knew as much about you as I wanted to," I said, "but I did know that much."

"You're sweet," she said in a sour voice.

"Anyway."

"Anyway." She stubbed out the smoke, savagely, sending a scattering of ash across her black cocktail dress. "I thought at first, the past is the past. I thought he wanted to get together for old times' sake, say he was sorry about Daddy, something like that. We did have some good times, once upon a time, you know. Like you and me."

I gave a little bark of a laugh. "Maybe not just like you and me. But...yeah." It somehow hurt to look at her, and somehow it was easier to study Aleksei's stiffening corpse.

"Sure," she said, seemingly unperturbed. "Anyway, he thought he was giving me a gift when he said that this house was in my name. And I saw it happening all over again—me fronting for him, playing the perfect hostess, while he ran coke and Vancouver girls fresh off the boat from China through here for his 'gentlemen's parties.'" She made quote marks with her nicotine-stained fingers before fishing another cigarette from a pack on the kitchen counter. "Fool me once, shame on me. Fool me twice, fuck you with a sandpaper strap-on."

My head jerked at that. Abby was no stranger to creative profanity, but the creative profanity I'd known her to use had a fun, bawdy quality to it; the product of a person enjoying herself and the world in all its wonderful ridiculousness, like I imagined a modern-day Audrey Hepburn would be. Was she really that cynical now? Had the years changed her that much? It seemed impossible to see her now and see the girl who used to say "fuckamonkey!" in playful exasperation over a particularly stubborn calculus problem.

"And so," I said, looking back at her unwillingly, almost afraid to hear the rest.

"And so, he laughed. Like it was a done deal and me resisting it was just a tiresome scene he had to let me act out. Before he had to 'take me in hand.'" Again with the finger quotes, and again with the tumble of ash. "'Take you in hand' was one of his favorite sayings, like he was fucking Cary Grant putting up with some silly screwball dame until it was time for a man to do what a man's gotta do, which was put a woman in a woman's place, because in the end, in this fucking Trumpworld we're in, it's a man's world, isn't it?"

She lowered her head, peered at me as if over glasses. "Can I just tell you that I am so fucking tired of fucking men?"

"I get that," I said. But I didn't, not really.

"And so. I said some things. He said some things back. Then his hands started doing the talking."

I looked back at the body, then again at her. At the dark circles that, upon closer inspection, revealed themselves to be bruises.

"And so," she said.

"And so," I repeated. "You need me to help you clean up. Get rid of the body. Because I work with blood. Because, you figure, I know how to do this without leaving traces of you behind."

She frowned at that. "Well...yes. But not just that. Because you love me, and because I trust you to do whatever needs to be done."

I swallowed, stared at the floor. "Do...you love me?"

She turned her face to the side a little, while giving me her eyes in full for the first time tonight. "In my way."

"But I'm here to help clean up."

"In a way."

I stood straight. Took a step back. "What do you mean?"

She went silent for a few seconds. Then pointed down toward Aleksei's bent left leg. "See that there?" She took a few steps forward, toward the edge of the tacky blood pool. "I think that's a gun. Another gun. Isn't it?"

The smell was starting to get to me, but I stepped forward too. "Yeah, looks like it. Hang on." Finally, something I could do. I pulled open a kitchen drawer and found a pair of salad tongs. I bent, stretched, and hooked the weapon by its finger guard. In a moment I had it wrapped in a dishtowel.

"Can I see it?" she asked. I handed it over. She went to the sink, ran some hot water, and wiped the gun clean with another dishtowel.

"What did you do that for?" I asked.

"I need you to handle this for me." She held out the dishtowel. Her eyes didn't quite meet mine. After a long silence, I took the dishtowel, and took the gun in my hand. I didn't know anything about guns except that I knew that I didn't like them, and I really didn't like holding this strangely malignant metal fist in my hand.

"You mean, you want me to drop this in the Sound or something?" I asked.

"Or something."

"I don't follow."

She stepped back, crushed out her latest Salem, and fiddled inside a black handbag that perfectly matched her perfect black dress. "I want to explain something to you. Something I've wanted to explain to you for seven years now." She looked away from me, out the kitchen window. "Remember that night when you bailed me out of jail? How you said you wanted to take care of me? Take care of things for me?"

I nodded.

"You were so...alpha. It was wild. A whole new you. It was...seductive. And for a second there I saw myself doing it. It would have been so easy. Letting you manage my life. Like Aleksei, without the criminal bullshit."

A few seconds ticked loudly between us.

"But then I saw it for what it really was. You wanted to possess me, didn't you? You wanted to take advantage of our friendship, of a weak moment in my world, and be just another guy who wants to call the shots for me."

"No—" I said. Then stopped. Because, I didn't know. Did I? I did, but—"I loved you," I said.

"Bullshit. You *fetishized* me." Her words hit me like the snap of a whip. "And in that moment, I knew it was all over. Our friendship. Because it never really was, was it? You were just lying in the weeds like all the rest. Like Aleksei. Just waiting for your moment. To pick me off like some wounded antelope on fucking *Animal Planet*."

"No," I breathed.

"Yes," she said, and her voice was steady. Dead steady.

"I don't understand," I said. "What are you—why did you do what you did, then? You know, at the lake? I didn't ask you to do that."

Her face filled with blood so hot it looked black.

"Because it was the only way to shut you up! To shut you *down*! To misdirect your tiny fucking male mind for two fucking seconds!" She made a savage swipe at the ashes clinging to her cocktail dress, and when she spoke again, her voice had regained that deadly lower register that I liked even less than the shouting.

"So I could breathe. Think. Regroup. Get back in my right mind. I could never have done that with you, because as tough as you thought you were, you're not, really. If I didn't know it for sure then—and I did—I sure as fuck know it now. I mean, really, Donny, look at your life. I saw your engagement picture online. You looked like you wished someone would do you the biggest favor of your flaccid little life and shoot you in the face."

I opened my mouth to say something like *That's not true* or *You don't know me anymore*. But nothing came out. I didn't have the lie in me.

She smiled. The sort of smile I sometimes saw on Thuy's face after one of our egg-timer coital appointments. *That was so good, baby. You do me so good. Good job, Donny.*

"To surrender to you would have been surrendering, period. And I don't surrender. Not to harder men than you. Not to any man. Not anymore."

There was a sick little scraping sound on the floor. I looked down in time to see a minute contraction in one of Aleksei's legs. Rigor mortis. Like the kind I'd been going through for seven years.

I shrank back for a second, and snapped back about as soon, and I heard Abby laugh. It was the sound of someone scraping away battleship gray from the inside of my skull.

"I'm sorry," I said. I set Aleksei's gun on top of the stove and turned away from her, for the coat I'd shrugged over a barstool when I first followed her into the dining room. "I'll just go. I do love you, you know. And I would never say anything, never do anything to hurt you. I'm sorry if that's what I did.

"As far as I'm concerned, this is an act of self-defense. Isn't it?" I put on the coat. "I thought I was here to help, but—"

"You are," she said, and when I turned to her again, I saw her holding a handgun, a smaller one. I couldn't form a single coherent thought.

"You heard I was back in town." She held the gun steady, in my general direction, as she shook her last cigarette out of the pack and touched it to her lips. "You were so obsessed with me, still, after all these years, that you dropped everything and ran out on your fiancée to find me. Meanwhile, I told Aleksei about you, my best friend in college way back when, and he beat your number out of me and made me call you, made me tell you where to find me. Because he doesn't believe in best friendships between men and women." She leaned back against the counter and looked down at Aleksei's legs. "Like you. I know you think you do, on some level, but deep down you know better, don't you? That all you really dream of is just being another fucking dude?"

That postscript hit me like, well...a pistol shot. I glanced at the gun I'd just set down. Stepped away from. Why had I done that?

"So. He attacked you as soon as you came in. I jumped on him, knocked him down, managed to get him to drop the gun. It flew toward you. You picked it up. He laughed. The big bad Russian gangster." She tried on a Boris Badenov voice: "You're not going to shoot me."

She smiled, a sleepy-eyed stretch of the lips. "But you did. Because once in a blue moon, you have yourself an alpha-dude moment, don't you, Donny?

"Only you were so shocked at what you did that you didn't quite have the presence of mind—the nerve—to finish him off. So he pulled a second, smaller gun from that holster on his ankle and shot you." She gave a ghoulish stretch of her lips. "Before he died, that is. Before I could call nine-one-one. From massive loss of blood."

"There's a problem with your theory," I said, and glanced again at the gun on the stove. Maybe twitched a little toward it, I don't know.

"Of course you'd say that. I'm so fucking tired of men thinking they know better than me. What's better *for* me. When I'm usually smarter than they are. What's the saying? God gave man two heads, but only enough blood to use one at a time. Thank you for showing me the true color of your blood once more, Donny." Abby lowered the cigarette and leveled the gun at me. "As far as I'm concerned, this is just...a redistribution of blood. Like you said, just an act of self-defense. Another one. Like every other goddamned one."

I chuckled, not fully believing she would shoot me. I wanted to tell her. I wanted to say: I know better because of what I do, not because of what genitals I have.

Any forensic pathologist worth their salt—male *or* female—would know from the blood samplings they'd surely take that Aleksei and I died at different times. If Abby tried to sell her story to any sheriff's detective with even a modicum of sharpness and a sanguine eye in the presence of a sultry female, she'd find herself back in the Whatcom County Jail faster than you can say, "Back, Jack, do it again."

And this time there would be no one to bail her out. No bail, period.

But.

She was a good hostess. A good brand ambassador to Club Abby, which never closes.

But, evidence. Even pretty women go to jail sometimes.

Or get someone to get them out of it.

Could she? No, the question was, *would* she?

I chuckled again, and it turned into a laugh. She laughed too. For the last time.

"This time," Abby said, "I'll work the flashlight *and* the shovel. These days, that's what a woman's got to do."

HALFWAY CRUCIFIED
Reed Farrel Coleman

Look, I know you're going to think I'm certifiable or full of shit. The few people I've told about this previously have either stopped talking to me altogether or treat me like their weird Aunt Claudette who talks to her porcelain doll collection, takes them with her to the mall in a stroller, and buys them all Häagen-Dazs. The people I've shared with who still deal with me are okay with me as long as the subject doesn't come up. On the rare occasion it does, they kind of smile and seem like they want to pat me on the head and say, "Take it easy, Ricky, it's nothing that a few years of shock treatment and psychotropics can't fix." I guess I can't blame them and their reaction is why I have never told anyone on the job. Yeah, can't you just picture the reaction of the other detectives at Brooklyn South Homicide hearing that I own a talking cat? That's right, he talks. It isn't telepathy. He doesn't scratch out words in his kitty litter. He speaks.

If it was only that Murray spoke, I suppose it would be difficult enough to explain. But what makes it worse is that Murray—a Siamese-Russian Blue mix—is smarter than any human I have ever met. And no, I don't mean that he's figured out how to open doors or how to lure unsuspecting birds into traps. I mean Mensa smart, like Einstein fucking smart. Besides,

Murray can't be bothered with feathers or raw meat. He prefers roasted chicken from the Stop'n'Shop deli. I didn't have to surmise his chicken preferences. He just told me the same way he told me his name.

When I brought him home from the animal shelter, I dubbed him Rasputin. Apparently, that pissed him off so much, it started him talking to me. Instead of looking up at me with little blue kitten eyes and mewing, he said, "Listen, *putz*, my name is Murray. You call me by that crazy anti-Semitic Russian's name again, I'll claw your balls when you're sleeping and give you such a lesson in adult circumcision you wouldn't forget." Murray speaks with a thick Eastern European accent and he's fluent in several languages. His favorite being Yiddish.

We don't discuss reincarnation anymore, because even Murray isn't smart enough to figure that one out. "Listen, *schmeckle*, it's pretty obvious I was once human and that God has a twisted sense of humor. You don't have to be a fancy NYPD detective like yourself to figure that out. Do I know who I was, exactly, or how I got to be a cat? Those are questions for felines above my paygrade. All I can say is that I'm glad that whatever I did to piss off the Almighty, it wasn't so bad that he brought me back as a dung beetle. Can you imagine the deep mysteries I'd be helping to solve or the conversations I'd be having? *Oy vez mir.* Even thinking about it makes my *kishkas* upset."

I thought it was cute that Murray called me *schmeckle* right up until the minute he informed me that it wasn't a term of endearment, but translated into him calling me a dick. He says there are an endless number of words for penis in Yiddish and that *schmuck, putz, schmeckle,* and *schwanz* are only a good start. These days I just assume that whatever Yiddish term he uses when he wants to get my attention is some insulting form of the word. But the roasted chicken bills and the insults are worth it because Murray is the best damned detective ever. Once, when I made the egregious mistake of telling him that I had been lucky to pick him out of all the kittens at the shelter, he coughed up a hairball onto my bare foot.

"I picked you, *schmuckalovitz*, not the other way around. I saw you show your shield to the chick at the shelter when you were trying to impress her. So I mewed at you and put my little furry paws up on the cage when you walked by and acted all sad, purred when you cuddled me. In my old life I bet I was quite the charmer. As a cat, it comes with the territory. And just between you and me, *boychik*, women who work at animal shelters are immune to the charms of policemen."

I had to admit, he was right about that. I think she was digging me until I flashed the tin. After that, I was lucky she deigned to let me adopt a cat.

"I guess you can have him," she'd said, giving me the death stare. "That kitten does really seem to like you."

I'm not sure that in Murray's old life he was a charmer. In fact, he was likely as big a pain in the ass as a human as he is now. His was probably the grandpa's house none of the grandkids wanted to go to on Sunday afternoon. *Do I have to, Ma? I would much rather stay home and read the entire collected works of Edmund Spenser in the original Middle English or I can just stick needles in my eyes.*

And true to form, Murray refuses to speak to anyone but me. "What, you think I want be a freak? I don't want I should be on late night television or anything like that. Look, already I must've done something that didn't make God very happy with me. I don't think he would want I make a celebrity of myself. This must be something like you *goyum* believe in, penance. Jews, we don't have Hail Marys or Our Fathers to get us off the hook. With you, Ricky, I do good. I find murderers. So, don't ask any more about why I don't speak with anyone else or I'll start pooping out of the kitty litter and marking my territory by going pishy all over the apartment."

But here's the thing about humans reincarnated as cats...or, at least about Murray. They are incredibly detail-obsessed.

This has its good and bad points. The good? Inevitably, in showing Murray my murder book, he sees something my partner or I have missed. On my last case, the brutal murder of an elderly woman staged to look like a robbery gone wrong, Murray saw a detail in the crime-scene photos that was so insignificant to me that I'd hadn't even noticed it.

"That pen on the floor," Murray said, "the one behind the radiator. Where's it from?"

"What pen?"

"*Oy gevalt, schmecklehead.* Look! Look!" He tapped his left paw on the photo.

He was right, there was a pen lodged against the wall and between the ribs of the old cast iron radiator. It was in an upright position, so that it was nearly impossible to see. He explained to me that a cat's eye view of the world would be very helpful for detectives.

"You can have all the fancy-schmancy equipment and tests in the world, but what good is it if you only see the crime scene by looking down on things?"

Murray was right. I went back to the old woman's apartment and dug the pen out from behind the radiator. It was a pen from the Wayfarer Motel in Sheepshead Bay and it had the suspect's thumb print on it. He was arrested at a bus station in Dayton, Ohio. He was a professional killer brought in by the landlord to take care of the old woman who had stubbornly refused to leave the rent-controlled apartment she'd lived in for fifty years. When they got rid of her, the value of the building she lived in went up several million dollars.

That's the good side of Murray's obsessiveness. The bad side? It's twofold. One, he needs to understand everything he can. Two, he can be very literal. So while Murray is utterly Zen about the fact that he may never know how or why the Almighty made him a cat, he can't accept his inability to make sense of song lyrics. That's actually an understatement. Not only can't Murray accept his inability in this area, but it makes him psychotic.

I discovered this phenomenon completely by accident. It was a very hot summer's day, a perfect beach day, and I had the windows wide open. Squeeze's "Pulling Mussels from the Shell" was blasting on the radio from the neighbor's backyard. Murray went, for lack of a better term, batshit crazy.

"What does it mean? What does it mean?" he kept asking me. "Who's Harold Robbins and what does a chalet and William Tell have to do with a beach? Why would Maid Marian stand on her tip-toed feet? And what does any of it have to do with mussels?"

When I shrugged my shoulders and said that it was just a song, Murray tore around the apartment, shredding the curtains, climbing the wallpaper, eventually diving into the toilet bowl to calm himself down. Even after I rescued him from the toilet, dried him off, and made him comfortable, it was obvious that Murray wasn't himself. I ran him over to the vet.

The vet called me into her office. "I've sedated Murray," she said. "His blood pressure and heart rate were extremely accelerated. Do you have any idea what caused him to react this way?"

Song lyrics. "I think he must've seen a dog or a possum or something and he just went crazy." I lied. "Maybe it's the heat."

She shook her head. "Yeah," she said, "maybe it is the heat. I think it must be getting to me, too. While I was preparing Murray's injection, I thought I heard an old Jewish man singing a Squeeze song. It sounded like it was coming from the examination room, but Murray was the only one in there. I guess I've been working too hard."

After that incident, I was careful to never play the radio in Murray's presence and had taken to very carefully screening the music I played in the house. And I made damn sure to never play any Steely Dan in the house. They'd been my favorite band in college, but I had long since moved in a somewhat different musical direction, one the Dan would surely have approved of. I was mostly a jazz guy these days. Lucky thing, too, given Murray's mania. I had spent many a long winter night at SUNY Plattsburgh, drinking Molson and Southern Comfort and philosophizing on the meaning of Steely Dan lyrics. There was one thing for sure, if Murray ever got hold of the Steely Dan songbook or their CDs, he'd be a goner. There wouldn't be a toilet bowl deep enough or curtains tall enough for him to work out his psychotic episode. Shit, I knew some humans whose obsession with Steely Dan lyrics had driven them to being institutionalized.

It had been about a year since Murray's Squeeze episode when I got the call from my partner, Leon Bates, to meet him at 74 Manhattan Court, two blocks from Coney Island Hospital. It was our day off, but Bates said the captain asked specifically for Leon and me. I knew it had to be serious for the captain to trash the rotation to ask for us. We were already less than popular with the other detectives in the squad because of our success rate and this wasn't going to make us any more well-loved.

When I turned off the Ocean Parkway service road onto the block, I knew it was trouble. Not only were the ME's meat wagon and the CSU van on site, but the captain's car was there as well. There were also some black Chevy Suburbans the Feds and the brass were so fond of. Manhattan Court was one of three blocks in an old garden apartment complex. I wasn't sure why they called them garden apartments, because the ugly little brown patches in front of each address barely qualified as dirt, let alone a garden.

Leon met me at the crime scene tape, handing me a pair of gloves. A uniform from the Six-One precinct took my name to keep a record of all the people who had access to the crime scene. Young, bright, African American, and ambitious, Leon was a real up and comer in the department. The brass had him penciled in for bigger things and so did he. His rep hadn't been hurt any by our closure rate, which hadn't been hurt by my adopting Murray. But even before Murray came into my life, we were a pretty good team.

"What's the story?" I asked, slipping into the gloves.

"McClatchy's here."

Dean McClatchy was the Chief of Detectives and he didn't make a habit of showing up at just any murder scene unless there was potential for heavy media coverage, good or bad. Still, his presence wasn't completely out of the realm of the usual.

"FBI, too," Leon said. "I think they're profiler types."

"That can't be good. Victim?"

"Peter Wallace, twenty-nine, white, single. Mental health aide at Coney Island Hospital. No criminal record. Lived here for five years."

"And what's all the excitement about?"

Leon shook his head. "You'll see soon enough."

Bates was right, because the moment I stepped through the first-floor apartment's door, I got the point. An eight-foot-high wooden cross had been affixed to the living room wall and Peter Wallace's body was affixed to the cross. But here's the thing, only Wallace's left arm and right leg were nailed to the cross. His right arm and left leg simply dangled. It might've been that the killer ran out of spikes or was scared off before he got to finish, but I didn't think so. The way Wallace's body was left seemed more like sculpture than serendipity. He was being presented to us, but I didn't know why. You're a homicide detective long enough, you get a sense of these things. You get to understand the difference between rational and random. I kept my thoughts to myself.

When I entered the room, the people standing around Wallace's body turned to stare at me. I recognized Chief McClatchy, the guy from the ME's office, and the crime-scene crew. It was the two white guys in the suits who were unfamiliar. Their condescension and superior attitudes were so intense I could smell it. I took a shot at humbling them before they started in on me.

"He was dead before he was displayed that way," I said, dispensing with the introductions or the small talk. "There's almost no blood around the spike wounds in the wrist and ankle. And even the pliable vic isn't going to just cooperate as spikes are being through his body parts. So what's the COD?" I asked the ME's man. "How long ago?"

"Twenty-four hours. Rigor has run its course. Cause of death? There are ligature marks around the neck, reticular hemorrhaging...I'd say strangulation is the answer, but we won't know for certain till we get him on the table."

"Either the killer is a strong motherfucker or there was more than one," I said. "Not easy to lift two hundred pounds of balanced free weights. It's a lot harder to lift a body and a cross and hold it against a wall while you bolt the cross to the wall."

McClatchy smiled at the Feds. The Feds were unimpressed. I expected nothing less.

"Anything else?" I asked the ME guy.

He held up a plastic evidence bag. There was a coin inside. I held it up to the light. It was dull gold in color with what looked like Arabic writing on one side and a profile of a man on the other.

One of the FBI guys said, "I'm Special Agent Neer and this is Special Agent Muni. So what do you make of the coin?"

"A piaster," I said, "from the Ottoman Empire."

That impressed them. It would have impressed me, too, if someone else had seemingly pulled that answer out of his ass. No one asked how I'd recognized an Ottoman Empire era piaster. Good thing. Might've been a little embarrassing to explain that I'd gotten so high one night at college listening to Steely Dan's *Katy Lied* that I went to the library and did research on piasters. Then it hit me. It hit me hard. The killer or killers were fans of the Dan.

The FBI guys must have seen it in my expression. Special Agent Muni said, "There's something written on the wall of the stairs leading to the second story apartment. It's directly behind the cross."

I got lightheaded, but I was sure I knew what it said. "You want me to guess?" I asked.

"Sure," said Neer.

"It says something like, 'On the other side of no tomorrow.'"

"Holy shit!" McClatchy couldn't contain himself.

Leon Bates choked like he'd swallowed his tongue, but the Feds just looked at each other and nodded.

"Will you come with us, Detective Collins?"

Leon looked pissed, but what could I do? I shrugged at him and mouthed that I would keep him in the loop.

A half-hour later, I was sitting in a situation room at the FBI offices in lower Manhattan. Neer and Muni and their boss, Supervisory Special Agent Larkin, stayed in an adjoining office while I studied the material I'd been given. In front of me were six sets of crime scene photos that were eerily similar to what I'd found at 74 Manhattan Court. The reports from the local police and FBI field offices were laid out for me to read. The first murder had been of a thirty-five-year-old cab driver named Marcus Davidson in Modesto, California and the last one prior to Wallace was a forty-year-old truck driver in Hershey, Pennsylvania named Amos Ritter. All the vics were just ordinary guys and, if you included Peter Wallace, the first letter of the victims' last names spelled D-O-C-T-O-R W. Each crime was committed exactly thirty days apart. It was pretty obvious to me and to the FBI where the killer or killers were going with this.

It was about four in the morning when I knocked on the adjoining office door to let Neer, Muni, and Larkin know I had finished looking through the files.

"Let me guess," I said, "You call the unsub Doctor Wu?"

They all nodded.

"Why wasn't the NYPD notified about this? I never got a heads up."

Larkin made some noise about not knowing exactly what to tell local law enforcement. "What were we supposed to tell you guys to look out for, a carpenter or circus strong man who targeted regular guys and who loved or hated Steely Dan? It would have caused more trouble than it would have helped. All we knew was that he was working from west to east."

I guess he had a point.

"So," Larkin said, "where's Doctor Wu going next?"

I laughed, because he knew what I would say. "Miami. But you can't do surveillance on every trucker, cabbie, or blue-collar guy of Cuban decent whose last name begins with U."

Neer said, "We know that."

Muni added, "That's why you're here. We know you've always been good at finding the thing everyone else has missed. We know there's something we're not seeing. It's there, but we're just not seeing it."

The problem was twofold: I wasn't the one good at seeing the thing everybody else was missing. That would be Murray. Second, I couldn't risk showing Murray the lyrics to "Doctor Wu". If "Pulling Mussels from the Shell" had driven him to dive into the toilet bowl and sing to the vet, I couldn't imagine what Steely Dan would do to him. But I had to try.

"Get me copies of everything and take me back to my apartment."

Murray could tell it was serious. Yes, Murray had his moments. He wasn't always a cranky old Jewish man trapped inside a cat.

"What is it, *boychik*? You look like your puppy died."

I explained the situation to him. He didn't react the way I thought he would. Instead, he went to his favorite spot by the window where he liked to sunbathe and watch TV. He washed himself from head to tail, including that cute thing he did where he licked his paws and then washed his ears. I was always curious about how that became instinctual to cats. When he was done, he trotted back over to me.

"Okay, *bubeleh*, obviously the big guy upstairs has a plan for me," Murray said, nodding up to the heavens. "And we can't just let another man get half-crucified because I got music issues. So here's what we're gonna do." He pointed his left paw at me. "You're going to that lady vet. She's hot for you, you know?"

"No she isn't."

"Don't be a *putz*, Ricky. She talks to me when she does her examinations and tells me things. Of course she thinks I can't repeat them, but we know better."

I wasn't pleased he had waited so long to reveal this to me. Dr. Sebastian was pretty hot and very kind. I'd been tempted to ask her out a few times, but Murray sort of complicates things. "So," I asked, "why are you just telling me now?"

"Because all she ever does is stick needles in me and shove a thermometer up my *tuchus*! But last time, when I went *meshugge*, she was really good to me. Believe me, from my point of view you never have to wonder why pets hate going to the vet."

"Okay, all right, so what's the plan?"

"They have cat Prozac," he said. "Get me some and little by little you'll introduce me to Steely Dan lyrics. I mean, there have to be some songs that aren't impossible to figure out, right?"

"Several," I said.

"Fine. We'll start with those. In the meantime, I'll build the Prozac up in my system and review the files. I figure within two weeks, I should be able to tolerate this 'Doctor Wu' song."

"How do I get her to prescribe it for you without bringing you there?"

"*Oy gevalt*, Ricky. Sometimes you really are a *schmuck*. Tell her I've started obsessively licking the same spots on my body so that the fur is gone and my skin is getting red. Tell her I'm pooping out of the litter and that I've become totally jumpy at loud noises. And if all else fails, ask her out."

Mission accomplished. She said yes to both. Murray had his Prozac and I had Dr. Sebastian. I was pretty worried when I brought her back to the apartment. Although Murray didn't talk to anyone else, he liked to play tricks on the women I brought home. I was concerned Murray might start singing "If I Were a Rich Man" or hide under the bed and speak in Romanian or Polish, but he behaved himself. The only uncomfortable moment came when Suzanne asked me to play some rock while we drank our wine. Since I'd stowed my old rock CDs away where Murray couldn't get at them, it was easy for me to lie to her and say I didn't really have any rock music. We made do with an old Weather Report CD I had around. Though she did seem curious as to why I didn't have Pandora, Spotify, Sirius XM or any downloaded MP3s.

"I guess I'm just an old-fashioned kind of guy," I said.

Her response: "We'll see about that."

We were rolling around the living room floor less than thirty seconds later.

When I got back to the apartment after taking Suzanne home, Murray said he was ready to give it a go. I dug out the CDs I'd lied about to Suzanne and Googled Steely Dan lyrics. Over the course of the next week we worked our way from songs with manifest content like "Kid Charlemagne" to "Dirty Work" to "Barrytown" to "Hey Nineteen" to more challenging songs that skirted the line between the obvious and the absurd. We had a few rough spots with "Brooklyn" and "Haitian Divorce." Murray kept getting caught up on how one drank a zombie from a coco shell. When I explained that a zombie is the name of a drink, Murray chilled, but he almost lost it with "Your Gold Teeth." I sacrificed another set of curtains on that one and it took a full day for him to recover.

Between the Prozac and gradual exposure, Murray had gained a real sense of confidence that he could make this work without going flip city. But I was circumspect, because I knew what lay ahead of us. In the meantime, Murray studied the files in the way only Murray could. I swear, it was like he could see individual pixels in photographs or spot the one word in a cop's note or a witness's statement that was the key to the solution.

By week two, the kitty Prozac had mellowed Murray out and he could listen to a whole Dan album without freaking. There were moments he'd pace or wash himself a little too much, but he was generally okay. Then, right in the middle of "Any Major Dude Will Tell You," he told me to shut off the music. I did so, fearing he was about to lose his shit. That wasn't it.

"How does Doctor Wu find his victims?" Murray asked. He didn't wait for an answer. "Get me the file on Jay Ormond."

Ormond was Wu's second victim. A devout Mormon, Ormond was a car wash manager in Salt Lake City. He seemed to have nothing in common with the others except in the most basic sense. He was a male between twenty-five and forty who had a blue-collar job.

When I got the file, Murray screamed at me to get out the crime scene photos. He shuffled through them and stopped when he got to one that seemed completely innocuous. Ormond's body wasn't even in the photo. It was a shot of Ormond's kitchen table.

"So what?" I said.

"*Vez mir!*" He shook his head in disdain. "How did you ever solve a crime without me? Look at the newspaper on the table. See, there's something circled in red in the paper."

I saw something was circled, but couldn't make it out. I went to my computer, where all the photos were in a digital format and could be manipulated. It was an ad for a local bar's karaoke night. I still didn't quite get it.

Then Murray recited, "'All night long, we would sing that stupid song. And every word we sang I knew was true. Are you with me Doctor Wu?' That's how he selects his victims. He travels west to east, going to local karaoke nights. If a man sings a particular song and the singer fits the right profile, he's a dead man. Go ahead, check with the FBI. I bet my whiskers and tail that every one of Doctor Wu's victims sang at a karaoke bar within a week of his murder. You just have to find out what song it is that all the victims chose. It's something about that particular song that stirs Doctor Wu's compulsion to kill."

Murray was right. Three days later, the FBI got back to me. Their field agents had re-interviewed friends, family, and co-workers of all the victims. They were indeed all karaoke lovers and they had all sung Emerson, Lake & Palmer's "Lucky Man." This confused Murray.

"This is a reason to kill someone? It's a nice song except for the static at the end, but a twelve-year-old could've written it."

"Murray," I said, "you understand a lot of things, but what drives people to kill can be very complicated."

As I—Murray, really—had broken the case, the FBI invited me to come down to Miami where they were setting the trap for Doctor Wu. They found a South Beach club that was willing to cooperate and paid to advertise a week of blowout karaoke nights leading up to Doctor Wu's kill cycle. I felt it was only right to bring Murray with me, but Neer and Muni told me that was a non-starter. I decided not to go. I liked catching killers, no matter who was ultimately responsible for finding them, but I didn't enjoy taking credit for work that wasn't mine.

Problem was, Murray and I must've missed something, because the killer didn't show up in Miami. Beginning on the twenty-fourth night of the cycle, I received a call from Neer. At first his tone was one of confidence tinged with mild disappointment, but with each night the confidence waned, the disappointment morphing into anger and desperation. On the thirtieth night, the kill night, Suzanne was over at the apartment. We'd ordered pizza and I'd bought a good bottle of Super Tuscan to complement the pie. The table was set and I was uncorking the wine when the apartment bell rang. Suzanne said she'd get the door and that the pizza was on her.

But when she came back down the hallway, she wasn't holding a pizza. A man the size of a mountain was holding Suzanne around the neck. He held a sawed-off shotgun to her temple. Suzanne was understandably panicked, struggling futilely against the big man.

"Doctor Wu," I said in as calm a voice as I could manage, hoping to get a reaction out of him.

All he did was squeeze Suzanne's neck so hard that she passed out from lack of oxygen.

"I saw you on Manhattan Court," he said in a cold monotone. "From an apartment across the street. You still haven't found that couple's bodies. I read about you, a regular Sherlock Holmes. Time to die, Sherlock."

"You were going to Miami. What stopped you?" I asked.

"God," he said, as if that was answer enough. I guess for him, it was.

"Let her go." I knew it was a waste of time, but I had to try.

He shook his head and clicked back the hammers on the shotgun with his huge thumb.

That's when Murray leapt onto my shoulder and sang, "He had white horses and ladies by the score. All dressed in satin and waiting by the door."

The mountain's eyes got wide and he let Suzanne drop to the floor, but he still hadn't let go of the scattergun. "Your cat is singing!"

"I know, but he only does ELP songs. Do you know how

many times I've had to endure 'Karn Evil 9' and 'The Sheriff'?"

Murray jumped off my shoulder and kept singing, "White lace and feathers, they made up his bed."

The big man's eyes followed Murray as he moved to my left. That was just enough time for me to grab my off-duty SIG from my ankle holster. As curious as I was about the big man's pathology, I didn't hesitate. Doctor Wu was dead before he hit the dining room floor. It was the first time I'd drawn my weapon in anger since my days in the bag. First time I ever fired my weapon at anything other than a target. I don't give myself a lot of credit. Doctor Wu was so big, I couldn't have missed him. While I attended to Suzanne, Murray called nine-one-one.

When Suzanne stopped clutching me, she looked into my eyes and said, "Is it true that he only sings ELP songs?"

"You heard that?"

She smiled. "The end part, yeah, while I was coming to."

"No, he actually doesn't usually sing at all. He just talks a lot."

"Good," she said, "because if he only sang ELP songs, I'd have to break up with you."

"We wouldn't want that."

"So that day last summer—"

I nodded. "Uh-huh, that was Murray singing."

"Thank you, Murray, for saving my life," she said.

He waved his paw at her. "It was him, Mr. Fancy Detective over here who did the tough part."

To this day, Doctor Wu remains a John Doe. The FBI has never been able to identify him and no one has as yet come forward to claim his body. Special Agent Neer tells me that the Behavioral Science Unit believes that Doctor Wu's actions were the result of childhood trauma caused by the clash of British prog rock with American fusion rock. Sadly, Doctor Wu was only the first of several serial killers linked to Steely Dan lyrics. There's a killer operating in the south the Alabama field office has dubbed Deacon Blues and one operating in Wisconsin they call Charlie Freak.

But I own a talking cat named Murray, so who am I to disagree with anyone's theory about anything?

ABOUT THE CONTRIBUTORS

STEVE BREWER writes books about crooks. His most recent crime novel, *Cold Cuts*, was his thirty-first published book. His first novel, *Lonely Street*, was made into a Hollywood movie in 2009, and *Bank Job* is currently under film option. A former journalist, Brewer teaches part-time in the Honors College at the University of New Mexico. He and his family own Organic Books in Albuquerque's historic Nob Hill district.

W.H. CAMERON raises chickens in his back yard in Oregon, and coaxes unruly words into mellifluous sentences in his writing room. "Hey Nineteen" marks the first appearance of apprentice mortician Melisende Dulac.

Called "a hardboiled poet" by NPR's Maureen Corrigan and "the noir poet laureate" in the Huffington Post, **REED FARREL COLEMAN** is the *New York Times* bestselling author of twenty-nine novels. Beside his own series novels, stand-alones, poetry, essays, and short stories, he writes the Jesse Stone novels for the estate of the late Robert B. Parker. He is a four-time recipient of the Shamus Award for Best PI Novel of the Year and a four-time Edgar Award nominee. He is currently working on the prequel novel to director Michael Mann's film *Heat*. Reed lives with his wife on Long Island.

LIBBY CUDMORE is the author of *The Big Rewind*. Her short stories and essays have been published in *The RS-500*, *Memoir Mixtape*, *PANK*, *The Stoneslide Corrective*, *The Big Click* and many other places. As a music journalist, she has written for *Paste*, *Albumism*, *Vinyl Me Please*, *Consequence of Sound* and the Captain's Blog at YachtRock.com. At press time, she has seen Steely Dan/Donald Fagen/The Dukes of September a total of twelve times. Twitter: @libbycudmore.

AARON ERICKSON is a former US Army Airborne Ranger who has served multiple tours in Iraq and Afghanistan. "Don't Take Me Alive" is his first piece of published fiction. He is currently working on a post-military thriller, drawing upon his war-time experiences. He writes quite a bit about American football at 49erswebzone.com.

NAOMI HIRAHARA is the Edgar Award-winning author of two mystery series set in Southern California and one in Hawai'i. Her Mas Arai series, which features a Hiroshima survivor and gardener, ended with the publication of *Hiroshima Boy* in 2018. The books have been translated into Japanese, Korean and French. The first in her Officer Ellie Rush bicycle cop mystery series received the T. Jefferson Parker Mystery Award. She has also published noir short stories, middle-grade fiction and nonfiction history books. For more information, go to www.naomihirahara.com.

MATTHEW QUINN MARTIN is a competitive bagpiper, former Jeff Goldblum photo double, and occasional writer of books and movies. More at matthewquinnmartin.com.

RICHIE NARVAEZ is the author of the award-winning *Roachkiller and Other Stories*. His work has appeared in *Latin@ Rising*, *Plots with Guns*, *Long Island Noir*, and *Tiny Crimes*, among others. His debut novel, *Hipster Death Rattle*, was released in March 2019.

Bestselling author of the Greywalker paranormal detective novels, **KAT RICHARDSON** lives in Western Washington, writing and editing crime, mystery, science fiction, and fantasy. She is currently the vice president of the Northwest chapter of the Mystery Writers of America. As a former journalist and editor, she has a wide range of non-fiction publications on topics from technology, software, and security, to history, health, and precious metals. A lifelong fan of crime and mystery fiction, and noir films, she is also the author of the Science Fiction Police Procedural *Blood Orbit* under the pseudonym K. R. Richardson.

PETER SPIEGELMAN is the Shamus Award-winning author of five novels, including *Dr. Knox*, *Thick as Thieves*, and three books—*Black Maps*, *Death's Little Helpers*, and *Red Cat*—that feature private investigator and Wall Street refugee John March. Peter's short fiction has appeared in many collections, including *Dublin Noir*, *Hardboiled Brooklyn*, *The Darker Mask*, and *Wall Street Noir*, a crime fiction anthology that Peter also edited. Prior to embarking on a career as a writer, Peter spent more than twenty years in the financial services and software industries, and worked with leading banks, brokerages and central banks around the world. He was born in New York City, where he currently resides.

JIM THOMSEN is a writer, manuscript editor and former newspaper journalist who splits his time between Florida and his hometown of Bainbridge Island, Washington. His fiction has been published in *West Coast Crime Wave*, *Shotgun Honey*, *Pulp Modern* and *Switchblade*.

BRIAN THORNTON is the author of eleven books and a whole bunch of short stories. His collection of three novellas, *Suicide Blonde*, is due out from Down & Out Books in late 2019. He does all of his own stunts, loves singing in the car with his son and the color blue, and lives in Seattle, where he is currently serving his third term as Northwest Chapter president for the Mystery Writers of America. Find out what he's up to at brianthorntonwriter.com.

JIM WINTER is the crime-fiction nom de guerre of science fiction writer TS Hottle. As Jim, he wrote the Nick Kepler series and the standalone caper *Road Rules*. His first novel,

Northcoast Shakedown, has been recently re-released. You can find this, as well as his ruminations on writing, rideshare driving, and music at jimwinterbooks.com. For his otherworldly stuff featuring ray guns, explosions, and aliens in space, go to tshottle.com. He lives in Cincinnati with his wife, Candy.

BOOKS

On the following pages are a few
more great titles from the
Down & Out Books publishing family.

For a complete list of books and to
sign up for our newsletter,
go to DownAndOutBooks.com.

Die Behind the Wheel
Crime Fiction Inspired by the Music of Steely Dan
Edited by Brian Thornton

Down & Out Books
978-1-64396-016-6

What's the end result of a crazy scheme to match some of music history's most evocative and memorable songs with twelve of today's most entertaining writers? You're looking at it.

With this collection there's no need to chase the dragon, tour the Southland in a traveling minstrel show, or drink Scotch whiskey all night long. You've already bought the dream.

Covering every game in the Grammy-winning catalog of Donald Fagen and Walter Becker—collectively celebrated as Steely Dan— these compulsively readable stories will stagger the mind of ramblers, wild gamblers, and—of course—the winners in the world.

¡Pa'que Tu lo Sepas!
Stories to Benefit the People of Puerto Rico
Edited by Angel Luis Colón

Down & Out Books
October 2019
978-1-64396-042-5

Join Angel Luis Colón and 11 stories from veteran and new-comer Latinx authors who need to be on your radar, *¡Pa'Que Tu Lo Sepas!* is a loud and proud celebration of Latinx writing, joy, trauma, and most of all, love.

Contributors: Chantel Acevedo, Hector Acosta, David Bowles, Hector Duarte Jr., Carmen Jaramillo, Jessica Laine, Richie Narvaez, Christopher Novas, Cina Pelayo, Alex Segura, and Désirée Zamorano.

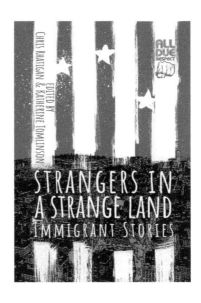

Strangers in a Strange Land
Immigrant Stories
Edited by Chris Rhatigan and Katherine Tomlinson

All Due Respect, an imprint of
Down & Out Books
978-1-64396-008-1

Strangers in a Strange Land: Immigrant Stories is an anthology that explores immigration in poems, essays, and short stories by a diverse collection of authors who offer their own experiences, observations, and speculations. From searing poetry drawn from a Native American perspective to essays chronicling the marginalization of LGBT people, to the crime fiction of new Americans and writers whose ancestors were brought to the country in bondage, this collection examines the intersection of hope and despair that defines the immigrant experience.

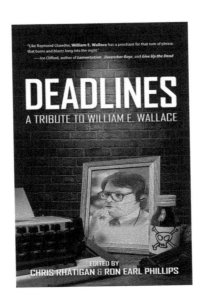

Deadlines
A Tribute to William E. Wallace
Edited by Chris Rhatigan and Ron Earl Phillips

A Joint Publication of Shotgun Honey and
All Due Respect, imprints of Down & Out Books
978-1-946502-48-3

Deadlines is a tribute anthology dedicated to the memory of writer and crime fiction enthusiast, William E. Wallace. All proceeds of this publication will be donated to the Comic Book Legal Defense Fund in the name of William E. Wallace.

Contributors: Preston Lang, Jen Conley, Joe Clifford, Will Viharo, Paul D. Brazill, Patricia Abbott, Rob Pierce, Sean Craven, Eric Beetner, Sarah M. Chen, Nick Kolakowski, S.W. Lauden, Scott Adlerberg, Gary Phillips, Renee Asher Pickup, Eryk Pruitt, Todd Morr, Travis Richardson, Anonymous-9, Sean Lynch, Alec Cizak, Greg Barth, C. Mack Lewis.